Debbie Johnson is a bestselling author who lives and works in Liverpool, where she divides her time between writing, caring for a small tribe of children and animals, and not doing the housework. She was a journalist for many years, until she decided it would be more fun to make up her own stories than to tell other people's. After trying her hand at pretty much every genre of writing other than westerns and spy dramas, she has settled on women's fiction that seems to make people laugh and cry, often at the same time.

Follow her on Twitter @debbiemjohnson

Or on
www.facebook.com.debbiejohnsonauthor
— but be warned, she mainly talks about dogs.

CHRISTMAS AT THE COMFORT FOOD CAFÉ

Becca Fletcher has always hated Christmas, but she has her reasons for being Little Miss Grinch. Now, though, she can't avoid her version of ho-ho-hell, because she's travelling to the Comfort Food Café to spend the festive season with her sister Laura and her family. She's expecting mulled wine, twenty-four-hour Christmas movie marathons, and all kinds of very merry torture. Little does Becca know that the Comfort Food Café is like no other place on earth. Perched on a snow-covered hill, it's a place full of friendship, where broken hearts can heal and where new love can blossom. It's where Becca's Christmas miracle really could happen — if only she can let it . . .

DEBBIE JOHNSON

CHRISTMAS AT THE COMFORT FOOD CAFÉ

Complete and Unabridged

CHARNWOOD
Leicester

First published in Great Britain in 2016 by
Harper*Impulse*
an imprint of
HarperCollins*Publishers*
London

First Charnwood Edition
published 2017
by arrangement with
HarperCollins*Publishers*
London

The moral right of the author has been asserted

This novel is entirely a work of fiction. The names, characters and incidents portrayed in it are the work of the author's imagination. Any resemblance to actual persons, living or dead, events or localities is entirely coincidental.

A catalogue record for this book is available from the British Library.

ISBN 978–1–4448–3500–7

Author Note

For those of you who have already read (and hopefully enjoyed!) *Summer at the Comfort Food Café*, the majority of the characters in this latest book will be familiar to you. Old friends, even. For those of you who haven't, don't worry — this one will still make sense. At least, that's the plan! While summer at our beautiful beachside café in Dorset focused on the story of Laura and her children, Nate and Lizzie, and was told from Laura's perspective, this story is told by her sister, Becca. We only met Becca via phone in the first instalment, but she was always one of my favourite characters — I hope you enjoy meeting her in person, and seeing the Comfort Food Café through her very different eyes. Becca's not always as easy to love as Laura — but she's always fun!

PART 1

Christmas Past: the Fletcher household, Manchester

1

December 25, 1987

Fizzy, the Twinkle-Eyed My Little Pony, is a rare and beautiful creature. She has a turquoise body and pink eyes and a silky-soft flowing mane. Fresh out of the box that morning, straight from Santa, she should be galloping across the matching My Little Pony duvet cover that is spread over Laura's single bed.

She should be neighing and singing and giggling with her friends, Applejack and Lily and Starflower the Rainbow Pony.

Sadly, that isn't happening. Partly because Applejack and Lily and Starflower are floating around in the toilet, with soggy loo paper clogged up around their manes, and partly because Fizzy — and her twinkly eyes — is currently being used as a weapon of mass destruction.

Laura's little sister, Becca, is four. Laura, being a much more mature six years old, always tries to be patient, because that's what her mum says she needs to be. And every time she's patient, she gets an extra sticker on her star chart, and once it's full, she will get a new Care Bear. Maybe the one with the rainbow hearts; she hasn't decided yet.

Becca has a star chart too, but hers is empty. Mum says it should be in 'negative numbers',

3

whatever that means.

Sometimes, Laura thinks, Becca is just ... mean. And loud. And not very nice. Sometimes she makes it *impossible* to be patient. Like now, for example.

Now, she's holding Fizzy in her chubby fist, and she's trying to hit Laura in the face with her, hooves first. Fizzy might be rare and beautiful and have a silky-soft mane, but nothing else about her is soft. She's made of plastic, and she really hurts when she's poked in your eye.

Laura had come up here to play while Mum was cooking the Christmas dinner and Dad was having a 'medicinal beer'. Becca had been crying and sulking all day, which he kept saying was because she was over-tired. He said it as though he felt sorry for her, and kept giving her hugs and carrying her around on his shoulders even when she was tearful and snotty.

Secretly, Laura didn't feel sorry for her. It was her own fault she was tired — she waited up until way past midnight, when the church bells rang out, because she wanted to see Father Christmas and Rudolph, even though she'd been warned that if she saw them, they'd never come down their chimney again.

Staying up so late meant she was grumpy and angry when they finally managed to wake Mum and Dad up, jumping on their legs in bed until they agreed to go downstairs and see if he'd been.

He had, and he'd left them loads of stuff under the tree — so Becca mustn't have seen him after all.

After everything was unwrapped, Becca had her own pile of toys — a Fisher Price kitchen and a koosh ball and a Play-Doh hairdresser set — but of course she didn't want to play with them. She wanted to play with Laura's. And when Laura said no, she screamed and grabbed a handful of the ponies off the bed, ran into the bathroom and threw them in the toilet.

She tried to flush them down but they wouldn't go, even when she poked them with that spikey brush Mum used to clean the loo with.

When Laura chased after her and tried to stop her, Becca snatched Fizzy out of her hand and started whacking her across the head with it. And it *really* hurt.

She'd tried to be patient, and she'd tried to be nice, and she'd tried to talk to her. But Becca just won't stop shouting and whacking, and Laura has had enough.

She grabs the shower attachment that is fixed to the bath with a big, bendy silver pipe, and turns on the cold tap. Not the hot one, because even if she is angry, she doesn't want any burny water spraying out. She points it at her sister and lets it blast full-force into her scrunched-up, furious face.

Becca's long brown hair is immediately plastered down over her cheeks, and the Strawberry Shortcake nightie she is wearing, the one that used to be Laura's, goes dark as the water spreads over it.

Her mouth is gaping open in shock, and her eyes are screwed closed against the spray. She drops Fizzy straight away and starts to scream. And scream. And scream.

Laura hears the kitchen door open downstairs and music wafting up from the radio that Mum always listens to when she's cooking. That song about China in your Hand.

There is a pause, and she knows Mum is standing at the bottom of the stairs listening to Becca screaming. Then the sound of footsteps coming up, and the door to the bathroom slamming open. By that point, Laura has dropped the shower head back into the bath, where it lies, twisting like a snake, sprinkling upwards into the sky.

She looks at her mum, guilt written all over her face, and feels tears sting the back of her eyes.

Her mum has tinsel wrapped around her head like a crown, and is wearing an apron in the shape of a fat Santa's body. There is a big wooden spoon in her hand, and she waves it threateningly in the air, as though she might use it like a sword at any moment. Her cheeks are red from the cooker, and there is dusty flour on her fingers.

'Can't you two play nicely for five minutes, for goodness sake?' she says, sounding as annoyed as she looks. 'All those new toys downstairs and you're up here arguing and fighting? It's not very Christmassy, is it?'

'Sorry Mummy,' says Laura, staring at her feet and trying not to cry.

'Aaaaaaaggh!' screams Becca, soaking wet and almost hysterical.

'I HATE Christmas!' she yells, pushing past her mum and her sister and squelching her way out into the hallway.

December 25, 1991

Laura decides that her mum is a bit drunk. Or 'merry', as her dad describes it, as they dance around the living room together, loudly singing along with 'I'm Too Sexy' by Right Said Fred. They are doing actions as well, pretending they are models strutting on a catwalk, and driving a car. Maybe Dad is a bit 'merry' as well, she thinks, watching as he tells the world that he is even too sexy for his shirt.

At the age of ten, Laura isn't quite sure what constitutes 'sexy' — but she hopes her dad isn't it. She also hopes they don't get so merry they collide with the Christmas tree, because the living room isn't really that big, and they don't seem to be entirely in control of their legs.

Becca sits in the corner of the couch, sulking as usual, rolling her eyes in a way that makes her look a bit like she's having some kind of seizure, and making gestures of glug-glug-glug with an invisible glass while she points at Mum.

That's because Mum had a bottle of wine open while she was cooking the Christmas lunch this afternoon, and said she needed it because 'the dragon-in-law' was visiting.

That's her nickname for Laura and Becca's grandma. She says she means it 'in a nice way', but she never says it to Nan's face, so Laura's

7

not altogether sure she does. Plus she stayed in the kitchen for ages, saying she was busy, but every time Laura went in she was just sitting at the table, muttering to herself, and pouring another glass. Grown-ups, she'd decided with David, were weird.

She wishes that David could have come over, but his parents have taken him away to Wales. Which is a whole different country and everything. She misses him, and hasn't even been able to speak to him on the phone to see what he got for Christmas.

He'd been hoping for a Gameboy, and had even carried on pretending he believed in Santa because he thought it would give him a better chance at getting one. Laura is also still pretending she believes in Santa, just because she thinks it makes her parents happy to think she does.

It had been harder this year, because Becca had finally decided that it was all made up. She stayed awake throughout the entire night, and all she heard, she said, was Mum and Dad going up and down the stairs, next door's cat yowling, and some random drunk people going past very late and setting off a car alarm.

Plus, Christopher Eccles at school — who had three big brothers — had laughed at her when she even mentioned Father Christmas. Becca wasn't keen on being laughed at, especially by Christopher Eccles, and she'd punched him in the face and run off to hide in the bike shed.

So now, Becca is mega-tired and in a mega-bad mood. Nan and Granddad have gone home, and Mum and Dad have decided to have a party of their own, and she's really annoyed that she got a Girl's World styling head and a Polly Pocket Country Cottage playset when she'd actually asked for nothing apart from Teenage Mutant Ninja Turtle toys — she'd drawn circles around them in the Argos catalogue and everything.

Laura has decided that the most sensible thing to do is ignore Becca and carry on making friendship bracelets from the set she got for Christmas. She plans to make one for David and one for Danielle and Sarah out of her class, and maybe — *maybe* — one for Becca too. Because leaving her out would be mean.

The music has changed and that Dizzy song is on now. Mum and Dad are whirling around, shouting about how their heads are spinning, and laughing out loud. Dad comes over and tugs Laura up by the hands, spilling her bracelets on the floor.

'Come on, join in!' he says, starting to spin her. 'It's Christmas! And it's *you* girl, making me spin now . . .'

Mum spins her way over to Becca, and tries to pull her to her feet as well. Becca doesn't want to join in, though, and instead she wriggles out of Mum's grasp and runs off up to her bedroom.

Laura doesn't hear it, because of the music and the dancing and the laughing, but she knows there will have been a door slam. Even at eight, Becca is really good at door-slamming.

By the time the song finishes and all three of them collapse onto the sofa, a bit sweaty and a lot happy, Becca storms back into the room.

'I didn't want this!' she yells, lobbing her Girls' World head onto the carpet. It rolls around for a bit, like a decapitated blonde, until it comes to rest beneath the Christmas tree, where it totters, red lips facing the ceiling. Laura sees that most of the shiny synthetic hair has been brutally hacked off, leaving bits sticking out in tufts, and that there are now just gaping holes where the eyes should be.

Becca stands in the doorway, hands on her hips, hair wild and tangled, brown eyes full of angry tears. She probably expected more of a reaction, but in reality, Mum and Dad are a bit too 'merry' to blow their top at her, even if she is behaving like a brat. A brat who likes killing blondes.

'Crikey,' says Dad, his chest puffing up and down after all the dancing. 'That'll be a good story to tell at your wedding.'

'I'm never getting married! And Santa doesn't exist, because if he did, he'd have brought me turtle stuff! And I HATE Christmas!'

December 25, 2000

There has been a lot of dancing in the Fletcher home this Christmas. The kids are older, and the fridge is well stocked with giant pork pies and Black Forest gateaux and multiple packs of lager, nestled next to Mum's Baileys.

Nobody gets out of bed at 5am to check for presents any more, and Dad doesn't have to spend the first half of the day with a screwdriver in his hand, searching for yet another pack of Triple A batteries.

The girls have their own rooms, so there is less fighting, and Laura has her own fiancé, which is a whole different story. David — the fiancé in question — has been at the house all day, with his Labrador, Jambo the Second. Even Jambo got in on the party, jumping up and down and woofing along to 'Who Let The Dogs Out?'

David and Laura did lots of joke-dancing to S Club 7 songs, and a smoochy to 'Never Had A Dream Come True', and Mum and Dad did mock line-dancing to 'Man I Feel Like A Woman', and everyone leapt around to Robbie Williams being a Rock DJ.

Everyone apart from Becca, that is. Becca had had a tough time recently. She'd split up with her boyfriend Shaun, and taken it hard. Nobody else in the family could quite figure out why she'd taken it so hard, as they'd only been together for a few months and always seemed to be arguing anyway. Even Laura couldn't get anything out of her, apart from a mouthful of bad language and a bedroom door slammed in her face.

But since the split, Becca had been sulky and sullen and had apparently forgotten how to operate a shower or use shampoo. Her skin was blotchy and sore-looking, her hair glued to her head with grease, and she spent as much time as she possibly could either asleep, pretending to be asleep, or, Laura suspected, indulging in substances — some legal, some not — that

11

would help her sleep.

She'd been dragged out of bed by their mum for Christmas lunch, and had sat at the table in her stained Eminem T-shirt, pushing her food around the plate and not actually eating any of it. She managed to drink, though — quite a lot.

By the time the dancing started, she was halfway to hammered, and she'd had enough. Of everything. Looking at Mum and Dad and Laura and David and even the bloody adorably cute dog was all just too much for her. They were like a scene from a film about happy families at Christmas, and she was the only one who didn't fit in. She was the evil Gremlin.

Becca didn't feel merry or jolly or thankful or festive. She barely even felt alive, and often wished she wasn't. It was like she was trapped in a bubble, on her own, completely isolated, even though she was in a room full of people who she knew loved her. In fact, watching them, seeing their happiness and their silliness, yet being unable to feel it herself, made everything so much worse.

She snuck out of the house mid-afternoon — seeing her dad gear up to do his rendition of Tom Jones' 'Sex Bomb' pushed her over the edge. She'd told Laura she was going round to her friend Lucy's house and she'd be back in a few hours.

She never made it to Lucy's house. She never intended to. She stopped off in the kitchen to raid the lager stash and headed on out without even getting her coat. That, she realised as soon as she made it outside, was bloody stupid

— there was snow everywhere. Laura and David had been so delighted with it, Mr and Mrs Perfect, yammering on about how pretty it was and laughing at Jambo snuffling in it and building snowmen together and having snowball fights like characters in some lame rom com.

They were just disgustingly good together, and it made Becca feel even more dysfunctional. Even more lonely. The coat, she decided, wasn't worth going back for. Not if it meant another dose of that kind of medicine.

Back inside the house, the party meandered its way through the rest of the day. There was more singing. More dancing. More eating. More drinking.

Laura texted her sister on her little Nokia mobile phone, and got a reply saying she was fine and would be back later. She wasn't completely happy with her being gone, but what could she do? Becca was seventeen. If she said she was fine, she had to believe her.

It wasn't until just after six in the evening that the bell rang.

Mum — a little the worse for wear after all her Baileys — answers the door, a glass in one hand and a slice of pork pie in the other. She's wearing a bright-green paper crown from a cracker, draped over her head at a wonky angle, drooping down to cover one eye.

The other eye can see perfectly, though. And what it sees isn't pretty.

There is a police car parked by the pavement at the end of the drive, its tracks perfectly clear on the snow-covered road. The flakes are still falling and the evening air is so chilly that Mum's breath makes a big, steaming cloud as she gasps out her shock.

One police officer is standing on the step, blowing into her hands in an attempt to warm them up, and another is walking towards them along the icy path. She has an arm around Becca's shoulders, and is half-walking, half-carrying her.

Mum rushes outside, lucky not to slip, and tries to help. There is a kind of tussle, where there are too many arms and legs flying around, and Becca is eventually safely deposited into the hallway, where she leans back against the wall and slides right down it until she is sitting on her bottom, legs splayed out in front of her.

'She's fine,' says the dark-haired policewoman, smiling through chattering lips. 'Just had a few too many, as well as being too cold. We found her in the park, sitting at the top of the slide. We put her in the back of the car to warm up and gave her a check-over in case she needed to go to A&E, but . . . well, who wants to go there at Christmas, right? We thought you'd probably prefer it if we brought her home instead.'

Mum nods her thanks, and Dad — who has made his way through to see what all the fuss is about, along with Laura and David and the dog — manages actual words. Mum mainly looks worried and Dad looks a bit angry.

'Don't be too hard on her,' says the police lady as she turns to leave. 'We were all young and stupid once, weren't we?'

Mum closes the door behind her and turns to

14

look at her younger daughter. Her big, stompy black boots are soggy and there is a distinct cigarette burn in her jeans that wasn't there before. Her eyes are half-closed, and Eminem's face is covered in what looks suspiciously like vomit.

Laura leans down towards her, strokes a strand of chilled hair away from her face, where it has become crusted to her cheek in some kind of lager-sick combo.

'Are you all right, Becs?' she asks, frowning in concern.

Becca slaps her hand away and belches loudly at her face. She turns her head, unsteadily, and manages to both sneer and cry at the same time. Bizarrely, the sound of a Christmas music show is wafting in from the living room, playing that year's number-one smash — 'Can We Fix It' by Bob the Builder.

Tears rolling down her blotchy skin, she lies on the carpet and curls up into a smelly, sad, foetal ball.

'Go away,' she says, through her sniffling. 'Just leave me alone. I hate you all. And I fucking well *hate* Christmas!'

PART 2

Christmas Present — Dorset

2

I have no idea when it was in my life that I had my backbone surgically removed. I was probably drunk at the time; entirely possibly stoned as well. Or maybe it was in 2002, when I tried (and failed) to go to Uni and instead spent almost a year locked in a bedsit in Bristol talking to a bonsai tree. The bloody thing never replied, which is, with hindsight, one of the few positives from that period of my life.

Whenever it happened, and whatever the circumstances, I have been rendered spineless. Devoid of vertebrae. I can't stand up for myself. I am incapable of resistance. It is literally impossible for me to say 'no'.

At least it is to my sister, Laura.

Laura is physically older than me by only two years, but by about three decades in terms of maturity. When we were growing up, she was always the good girl. The pretty girl. The one who everyone liked. The one my mum's friends would look at, and go 'aaah, isn't she gorgeous?'

I was the one they looked at and simply went 'aaaaagh!' — which is a fair reaction as I spent much of my childhood having screaming tantrums, stabbing people with forks, swearing and growling at the world like a mad dog who'd swallowed a whole nest of wasps.

I was not, to put it diplomatically, a 'pleaser'.

To be fair and accurate, my mum and dad

never loved me any less. They never locked me in a cupboard, or beat me, or threatened to send me away to Miss Hellish's Academy for Troubled Youngsters.

They displayed far more patience than I probably would if I had kids. Nothing they did ever made me feel like an outsider or like the odd one out — I was quite capable of doing all of that by myself.

So, Laura was the good one. I was the bad one. These were the roles we played, quite happily I might add, for most of our childhood.

We've joked about it since — about how occasionally, every now and then, one of us would slip up and act out of character. I would accidentally do something kind, or actually agree with my mum, or join in when the rest of them did the rap from the beginning of *Fresh Prince of Bel Air* instead of pulling a face and slamming the door as I exited the living room.

And even less occasionally, Laura would take on my role as the rebel. There was a time, for instance, that she forged my mum's signature on an absence note so she could bunk off school for the day with her boyfriend, David.

They went to see *Twister* at the Odeon; I remember this quite clearly because for days afterwards, they used to run around, ducking under tables and shouting 'Debris!' as though it was the funniest thing in the world.

And once she climbed out of my bedroom window, onto the garage roof and down the drainpipe, so she could sneak to a party with him.

And another time, she . . . well, no. She didn't. I've actually run out of bad things she did now, which I think means it comes to a grand total of two. She wasn't perfect — she could roll her eyes with the best of them — but neither was she difficult. She was one of those girls people liked; one of those girls whose mums could safely say 'she gives me no trouble' about, even when she was a teenager.

I, however, wasn't one of those girls. At heart, I was all right. I think my family always knew that, which possibly explains their superhuman patience levels.

I might have been vile on the surface, but underneath I always had a code. I never bullied anyone. I never hurt animals. I never stole. I did, however, turn the air blue with my language; drink to excess; buy and use recreational drugs; slack off at school; tell teachers and other authority figures to go f**k themselves on a regular basis; get piercings before everyone else did; dress like something from a horror film and hang around with a gang of other ne'er-do-wells who looked like the ensemble cast from a Goth version of *Prisoner Cell Block H*.

And while I was never the world's easiest to deal with — I'm even scowling in the baby photos — things got even worse after my seventeenth birthday. I hit a bit of a speed bump that year, which I don't like to dwell on, and took a sharp turn from surly-but-acceptable to call-in-the-exorcist-her-head-is-spinning.

As I delved even deeper into the abyss, finding brighter and shinier ways to hurt myself, Laura was busy planning her wedding. To David, the boy she'd loved since I was five years old and she was seven.

I know, it sounds crazy. It was crazy. It was as though everything between us was divvied out wrong. She got too much domesticity and no sense of adventure, and I got all the rebellion and fight. Between us, we'd have probably made one normal human being.

So, I was the bad one — and I slowly got worse, after that little speed bump I mentioned. The speed bump I didn't just hit, but that made me crash, somersault and burst into flames. Seriously, I was so messed up that if I was a car and not a human, they'd have taken me to the scrap yard and got me crushed up into one of those little rusty metal cubes.

My chosen methods of self-destruction tended to be booze and drugs and men, which resulted in more than a couple of trips to A&E, dropping out of college, developing a very on-off relationship with personal hygiene and several other behavioural traits that caused a lot of sleepless nights for the poor, driven-mad parentals.

While all of this was going on, Laura continued to be the good girl. Even though they were initially concerned about her settling down too young, one look at the shambles of my life was enough to make Mum and Dad happy that Laura was doing what she was doing. Heck, the shambles of my life made it look like head-shaving-era Britney Spears made good choices.

I chose chaos — she chose marriage and kids and being a suburban goddess. Or maybe those roles chose us. I don't really know.

As it turned out, though, the parentals have probably had just as many sleepless nights about Laura as they have about me now. Because her entire life fell to pieces a few years ago, when her husband, David — the beloved David of Myth and Legend, the boy who won her heart in primary school — died.

He died in a bloody stupid way that still makes me angry. He died falling off a ladder, while he was clearing leaves out of their guttering. It's not glamorous, is it? Nothing involving guttering ever could be. Or death, now I come to think of it. But at least members of the 27 Club exited this world in a cloud of mystique and self-indulgence. They weren't clearing leaves out of their damn gutters.

David was only thirty-three, the same age as Laura was at the time. He was too young to die, and she was way too young to be a widow. He left her on her own with their kids, Nate and Lizzie, and their dog Jimbo. He left her on her own, when she'd never been on her own before. While I'd lived my life on the margins of my own family, she'd gone off and created her own — one that revolved around the love story that she shared with David.

I can't begin to describe the hell on earth that followed his death. Mainly for Laura and the kids, obviously, but also for the rest of us. You can't see someone you love suffer like that and not go through it with them.

I watched her fade and struggle and fight and fade again, over and over, like some twisted Groundhog Day. I saw her try to be brave and I saw her collapse, and I saw her paralysed with pain so strong I honestly thought she'd never move again.

I saw her weep and I saw her tremble and, worst of all, I saw her silent — silent and withdrawn and empty, her face a blank mask, going through the motions of life and mother-hood, living on automatic pilot, functioning without feeling.

I saw all of this, and I saw Lizzie and Nate go through their own agonies, and I saw my mum and dad snarled up with their inability to do anything, and I saw myself, quietly screaming inside.

It was the very worst of times — and it seemed to go on forever.

Until, that is, she got her second chance. Until she applied for a job at a café in Dorset and took the kids down to the coast for a long, hot, working summer.

Until she made a world of new and wonderful friends and got a new dog, and found her new home, and found a man who is helping her heal. Until she found the will to live again.

Until she found the Comfort Food Café.

Which is exactly where I am heading this month — December. Against my will, I am being dragged away from the comfortable urban buzz of my flat in Manchester, and my shallow-but-safe existence and, more importantly, my entirely Christmas-free lifestyle.

I don't want to go, but Laura asked me to. And when it comes to her, I have no backbone. No spine. I simply can't say no.

I really, really hate Christmas.

But I love my sister more.

3

'Where are you?' Laura says, over the phone, her voice sounding strained.

'I'm in a Parisian brothel,' I reply, 'learning how to do a can-can that would make Craig Revel Horwood weep. It's fab-u-lous, darling.'

'I can hear lorries making that beeping noise they make when they're reversing. Are you at a service station? And if so, which one? If it's the one that sells Krispy Kreme doughnuts, can you bring us a box? And when will you be here? The kids are driving me nuts asking every five minutes . . . they won't even start decorating the tree until you arrive . . . '

I make a small grrrr noise at the back of my throat, like a grumpy grizzly bear, and wonder how she saw through that impeccably plausible can-can story. My sister, the mind reader.

Although if she really was a mind reader, she'd know that I was sitting here, drinking coffee in the freezing cold, shivering my backside off, and trying to think of a good excuse to turn the car around and head back Up North. It might be grim, but at least I wouldn't have to decorate a Christmas tree and pretend to be jolly.

Laura hears my little growl and laughs out loud.

'Not thought of a good enough excuse to get out of it, yet, then?' she says. Damn her. She *is* a mind reader.

'Not yet,' I reply, wrapping my hands around the paper of my coffee cup in an attempt to stave off frostbite. Christmas is not only annoying, it's cold as well. 'But I'm hopeful that there'll be some kind of natural disaster that splits the world in two before I reach Bristol. You know, like in one of those earthquake films, where a huge gaping chasm opens up in the middle of the road and all the expendable extras fall into it? Or possibly a zombie apocalypse. Or a meteor shower. I'm not fussy.'

I can hear yapping at the other end of the phone and smile as the sound is inevitably followed by Laura muttering 'hang on . . . ' as she scurries around, opening and closing doors, and otherwise catering to the needs of her newest baby — an eight-month-old black Labrador puppy called Midgebo.

He was originally Midge, and mainly still gets called that, but the 'bo' was added as tribute to all of David's dogs — also black Labs, and all called either Jambo or Jimbo.

Jimbo, the late, the great, the sadly departed, had gone to the great sausage shop in the sky not long after Laura and the kids moved to Dorset.

I knew she still missed him, but I also knew that Midge had helped to fill in the gap. As had Matt, the local vet who'd bought him for her. Matt, I suspected, was filling all kinds of gaps — and I was looking forward to meeting him. He looked a bit like Han Solo, so who wouldn't want to meet him?

I was looking forward to a lot about this trip. Like seeing my sister again and checking that her

27

apparent progress was genuine, not just faked for my benefit. Seeing my wondrous niece and nephew, who always made me feel glad to be alive. Seeing their new home. Meeting the famous Matt, and Laura's legendary boss, Cherie Moon, who owns the Comfort Food Café. Being introduced to all her new friends.

Yep, I was looking forward to a lot of it. I just really, really wished it wasn't at Christmas. It's never been my best time of year.

'Right. I'm back. Sorry about that,' she says, and I can tell from the change of background noise that she is now outside, probably watching Midgebo have a pee in the garden.

'That's okay. When a dog's got to go, a dog's got to go. Anyway . . . I should be there before dinner.'

'Assuming there isn't an earthquake or a zombie apocalypse, that is.'

'I think both of those suggestions are ridiculous,' I reply, standing up and throwing my empty coffee carton into the bin. 'But the meteor shower could happen. I think it was predicted on the weather last night.'

'Actually it was snow that was predicted,' says Laura, sounding distracted again. Having a puppy, I realise, is very much like having a baby.

'So drive safely,' she adds. 'Don't accidentally-on-purpose head back for Manchester. And don't forget the Krispy Kremes.'

4

I arrive at the Rockery, where Laura now lives, just as evening is drawing in. The promised snow has arrived, coming in small ineffectual flurries, none of which has settled. Half-hearted snow, really a very poor effort.

I was tired on the journey, and almost hypnotised by the sight of white flakes landing on my windscreen and promptly getting squished away by the wipers. It felt wrong somehow, like I was committing some random and callous act of snowflake genocide.

I know, when I start to have thoughts like these, that I probably need a good sleep.

It is strange pulling into the gravel-topped carpark at the cottages; an odd feeling of déjà vu, even though I have never been here in the flesh. As soon as Laura and Lizzie and Nate arrived here over the summer, Lizzie started taking pictures and posting them on her Instagram account.

As a result of living those months vicariously through social media, I feel as though I have been here before. That I've already seen the smooth green lawn and the little fountain in the middle of it. That I've already strolled past the individual cottages with their odd names: Cactus Tree and Lilac Wine and Poison Ivy. They're all named after bands or songs from the sixties and seventies, christened by Laura's former rock-chick boss and owner of the cottages, Cherie.

I feel as though I have already stood in this very spot, looking around at the snow-dusted trees and little patios and the dark, rolling hills beyond, but on much sunnier days. It was a scorching summer — destined to become one of those famous ones, talked about in the way my parents still do about 1976 and 1977, when there was a hosepipe ban and the Queen's Jubilee and Britain basically turned into the Med with strikes and bell-bottomed trousers.

Now, though, at the start of December, the sky is a dull gunmetal grey, patchy clouds marking it like bleach stains. The gravel is damp from the failed snow, and the cottages that are inhabited are lit up, bright lights shining from windows, curtains starting to be drawn.

It's still beautiful here, but not the oasis of wildflowers and birdsong that I have been pro-grammed to expect by my secondhand encounter with the place throughout July and August. Lizzie's Instagram pics have slowed down since she started to live here for real, so for me, it's a sudden jump from the height of summer to the bleak midwin-ter. It's odd, like I'm in a movie and we've just done a huge flash-forward.

I heft my bag over my shoulder, lock the car and enjoy a few more moments of solitude before I enter the cauldron of life that I expect my sister's cottage to be.

Don't get me wrong — I love that cauldron of life. I'm thrilled to be diving into it for a while. But I have lived alone since I was eighteen years old and have never shared my space as an adult human being. Not even with a cat, or a budgie.

I am used to solitude and it is used to me. We understand each other, me and solitude. I don't get annoyed when it keeps me awake at night with its echoing loneliness, and it's always cool about me sometimes bringing friends home to chase it away for a while.

Like a grumpy but dedicated couple, though, we always come back to each other at the end of the day.

Now, I am voluntarily putting myself in a situation where I will be surrounded by people for a whole month. People I love, admittedly, but still . . . it's not going to be easy. I have to be careful with myself, I know that. I have to watch my mental health, stay on an even keel, and try super-hard not to let things start to swamp me. Because not only are there all those people, but it's bloody Christmas as well.

I freeze on the spot for a second, feeling my resolve falter; feeling my fear start to twitch and flutter inside me like a moth trapped in my intestines. I could still escape, a little voice tells me. Me and my solitude could jump straight back into my bright-red Suzuki Swift (my Noddy car, according to my sister), and leg it up the motorway. There would be nothing left to show I was ever here. Well, apart from the Krispy Kremes. It'd be mean to take those with me.

I'm not really considering it, I tell myself. I wouldn't really do anything so insane. And yet . . . my fingers are gripping the car keys so hard I know they'll leave bright-red marks, and I'm chewing my lips, and I'm already planning the reverse route . . .

'Freeze!' says Laura, emerging from a path by the side of the lawn. She is pointing a finger at me like a fake gun and walking briskly in my direction. 'We have you surrounded; don't even think about making a run for it!'

I laugh out loud. I have to, really. She knows me way too well.

I plonk the doughnut box down on the roof of the car and meet her half way. We engulf each other in a big, comfy hug, and I feel at least some of the anxiety drain out of me. As soon as she has her arms around me, I wonder why on earth I was worried. Why was I feeling so crazy?

That, however, is the mystery of The Crazy, isn't it? It doesn't really make sense, or it would be called The Logical instead. And that wouldn't sound right — I mean, nobody ever spends a night with me and then says 'hey, you're such a Logical Bitch'. It's always the other one.

We pull apart and I get my first proper look at my sister. It is a look that makes me feel immediately much happier. We both have dark-brown hair, but while mine is long and straight; hers is wild and curly and all over the place. She dyed a strand of it bright pink over the summer — I suspect alcohol was involved — and that is partly grown out, but still there, flicking around vividly in the fading light.

She's wearing a pair of washed-out old jeans with grass stains on the knees and a huge baggy cardigan covered in tufts of dog fur and red-and-green striped socks with open-toed Birkenstock sandals. There is a smear of something that looks like icing on her cheekbone and I notice as she gets closer that one of her socks has a big hole in it, letting a pink-painted nail pop through.

Despite the disaster zone that is her outfit, she has never looked more radiant.

Her green eyes are bright and clear, her skin is smooth beneath her still-clinging summer tan and she literally can't get the grin off her face. She is sparkling, from the inside out, like Edward Cullen in sunlight.

She looks like the old Laura. The Laura who was happy. The Laura I knew before the imposter came, the fake Laura who was so smashed up by grief and longing that she was like a mutant, a hollow shell wearing a pale imitation of my sister's face.

I don't know whether it is the healing power of time, or her new job, or her new friends, or her new man, or just the sea air down in Dorset, but something has changed in her. It's been a long time coming, and it fills me with joy.

I pause, and say a little prayer of thanks to whoever the Supreme Commander in the Sky may be. I also throw up a little hello to David, the husband she lost. Because he, of all people, would be pleased to see this transformation — he would want her to be happy, I know he would.

Almost without me noticing, my eyes have filled up with tears, and I'm only alerted to the fact when a couple of them blob their way down my cheeks. An inappropriate response, I know — but that's kind of my speciality subject.

'You okay?' she asks, stepping back and giving

me some room. As I said, she knows me too well.

'Yes,' I reply. 'Just a bit freaked out. I've not inhaled traffic fumes for over an hour now. I think I'm going into some kind of detox.'

'Yeah. It gets you like that. Don't worry if you hear some strange noises, either. There's a cow near here that sounds like it's having a rave every night.'

'That sounds udderly terrifying,' I reply, giving her a wink. She groans, which is totally fair.

'Come on. The kids are about to explode.'

I retrieve the Krispy Kremes and follow her through, down the path, past the other cottages. I glance across as we near Black Rose, the big house on the corner where Matt the Hot Vet lives, and I see lights on in his windows. I imagine he is sitting inside, looking like Han Solo, playing the guitar while he single-handedly saves the lives of a litter of pug puppies.

'Is Matt in?' I ask, already knowing the answer. 'I should take him a doughnut and give him that Princess Leia outfit. There's nothing that says Christmas quite like a bit of sordid cosplay.'

It has been a standing joke between us since the two of them met that Laura should dress up in Leia's famous slave-girl costume. When I suggested this, months ago, I was simply being rude and provocative, which is often the case with me. But since their relationship took off, I got a bit more serious about it and ordered her one off eBay. It will be an amusing Christmas gift, if nothing else.

She glances at me over her shoulder and I see that she is smiling. Good, I think. Not only is it

34

all still going well, she's not even embarrassed about it.

'Maybe later,' she says. 'For the time being, you have to help the kids do the tree.'

I nod, but as soon as she turns away from me, pull a face that reflects my true feelings: I'd rather have a threesome with the Chuckle Brothers and a vat of olive oil than engage in such a horrendously festive act.

'And stop pulling a face,' she says, without even looking back. 'Christmas is all about the little ones.'

I resist the urge to point out that her kids aren't so little any more, as to mothers — including our own — we simply always are, no matter what physical evidence there is to the contrary. Lizzie is fifteen now, and Nate is thirteen. They are terrible teens, I think, as we approach Laura's cottage — Hyacinth House, named after a Doors track. They are probably only pretending to still be into Christmas to keep their mum happy.

As I walk through the cottage door, I am almost deafened by the sound of Christmas crackers being pulled, party poppers going off, and two excited children screaming in unison. I am immediately showered in bits of silly string, glittery streamers and handfuls of foil confetti.

'Happy Christmas, Auntie Becca!' they shout, rushing towards me and forcing a bright green paper hat onto my head.

Hmmm. So much for that idea. I am clearly alone in my hatred of all things mistletoe and wine.

I try to smile, because that seems like the proper thing to do in the circumstances, but I feel my face almost cracking in half with the effort.

I rub my eyes clear of the confetti, pull the thickest strands of silly string out of my hair, and look up at my niece and nephew and sister.

All three of them are also now wearing paper party hats and all three of them are creased up in hysterical laughter. Lizzie is holding her stomach, pointing at me and giggling so much she can hardly breathe. Nate is waving another party popper around like a machete and Laura is leaning against the wall, choking on her own guffaws. It would serve her right if she did.

'Oh gosh,' says Lizzie, straightening up and wiping tears from her eyes. 'The look on your face! Brilliant!'

'You are all,' I say, standing tall and using my very best Haughty Queen of Hearts accent, 'a frightful shower of bastards. Off with your heads!'

This provokes another round of laughter and it is so infectious that I am forced to join in. It might take me half an hour in the shower to get rid of all the crap I am now coated in, but I suppose, from their perspective — at a push and if I'm feeling generous — that their Christmas ambush was pretty funny.

In an act of mean-spirited but necessary revenge, I open the lid of the box of Krispy Kremes and proceed to take one big bite from every single one of the cakes. This is both childish and extremely satisfying, and by the time I dodge their attempts to grab them off me and flee with my mouth stuffed full of icing into the living room, I am feeling much better. A tiny bit sick, but much better.

The living room, I realise as I look around, is again both familiar and strange. Familiar, because Lizzie's summertime photos had already revealed it in all its chintzy, uber-floral, beamed ceiling glory. Strange because literally every available surface is now covered in Christmas decorations.

There are angels and snowmen dangling on strings from the beams, as well as a reindeer mobile where all the little plastic animals have flashing red noses. The glittery confetti in the shapes of trumpets and stars is strewn across the TV stand, the coffee table and the bookcase, and even in the strands of the fluffy rug.

The mantelpiece over the open fire is draped with fake holly boughs and fairy lights, and the whole room is dominated by the ridiculously large Christmas tree in the corner. It's a real one, not like the fake green thing we had as kids, and it looks like it's been donated by the King of Norway.

I feel my eyes widen as I look it up and down, and wonder if there are furry rodents nesting in there. It is, I see gratefully, already decorated, and that Laura had only been winding me up when she said the kids wanted me to do it with them.

The tree is a huge, messy confection of tinsel and baubles and lights and chocolates on strings, although only on the upper branches, which I suspect is down to the frequent visits of a Labrador puppy.

'Good, isn't it?' says Nate, sidling up to me and nudging me. I'm sure he actually wants a big cuddle, but is too cool to initiate contact. I'll get him later, catch him unawares when his guard is down. 'It's the biggest tree we've ever had.'

'That's because *Matt* chopped it down for us,' adds Lizzie, rolling her eyes; and adopting a sing-song Disney Princess voice. 'And Matt is the biggest strongest man in the whole wide world! And he has a magical axe! And he went into the haunted forest all alone, just for us, so we could have the most special Christmas *ever!*'

Laura sticks her tongue out at her, and I am impressed and relieved with how relaxed they are around each other. It's not just Laura who's changed, I think. It's all of them. For so long, before they left Manchester and moved here, everyone was walking on eggshells. Nobody wanted to upset any of them and they didn't want to upset each other, and the horrible end result was that absolutely everyone was upset all the damn time.

Now, I see them the way they should be. Happy. Loud. Rude. Perfect. If I have to tolerate a merry Christmas and spend the next month picking glitter off my clothes, it will be worth it just to see this.

I finally finish off the last mouthful of doughnut — some kind of white chocolate and raspberry, I think, but by this stage my tastebuds have all died — and smile.

'I thought you were waiting for me to decorate

the tree?' I say. 'Now I'm so disappointed. I've been looking forward to that all day . . . '

'We saved you the best bit, Auntie Becca,' replies Nate, grinning so hard I know something amusing is coming. 'It's a very special fairy we made to go on the top.'

Laura passes me a cone-shaped object that seems to be constructed from an old toilet roll tube and some paper doilies. The head is a battered ping-pong ball and glued to it, as its face, is a cut-out photo of me when I was about eight.

I recognise the picture. It was taken the year I caused a scene because I didn't get Mutant Turtle toys from Santa. Originally, it would have been of both me and Laura — her smiling like a perfect angel, of course, the bringer of joy. Next to her, I look like Satan's favourite stepchild, my face a picture of absolute misery. Seriously, it's a face that only a mother could love — and I'm not entirely sure my attitude at this time of year has improved very much at all.

I nod in recognition and announce, in a kind of Gandalf the Grey Setting Off to Mordor voice: 'I shall accept this sacred mission. Onward, to the top of the tree!'

I clamber up onto the dining table, realising once I'm up there that I can't stand straight or I'll bonk my bonce on the beams, and do a crab-like shuffle until I am perfectly positioned next to the enormo-tree.

I ceremoniously place the hideous me-fairy on the very top spikey bit, and manage to get down again without killing myself. This earns me a round of applause, and, joy of joys, a couple more party poppers get sprayed into my hair.

'Now, we can't wait to show you the rest of the cottage!' says Lizzie, enthusiastically. 'Everywhere is decorated — especially your room! That's the best of all!'

'Oh goody,' I respond, not even attempting to sound genuine now. The swines are doing this on purpose. 'I can barely wait.'

'Actually,' adds Laura, absently reaching out and picking random stuff out of my hair in a borderline invasive way that reminds me one hundred per cent of my own mother, 'we have a bit of a surprise for you on that front. Call it an early Christmas present, if you like.'

'Okay,' I reply, moving back a few steps to stop her fiddling. She immediately realises what she was doing and grins in apology. 'Hit me with it. Inflatable Santa in the bed? Live donkey by my manger? 'Now That's What I Call Christmas' 108 piped direct into my room through invisible speakers?'

'None of that,' says Laura, 'though they are all excellent suggestions, and I'll tuck them away for future use. No, the early Christmas present is a bit simpler than that — it's a place of your own to stay while you're in Dorset.'

'What do you mean?' I ask, frowning in confusion. The plan was always that I would stay in Nate's room and he would bunk in with Lizzie on a camp bed, sofa-surfing if she tried to kill him in his sleep.

'I mean your own flat. Des res, great location, magnificent sea views, and best of all, a totally

40

Christmas-free zone . . . '

'Cherie's apartment!' trills Lizzie, bopping up and down in anticipation.

I give her a sideways glance, wondering what's so exciting about Cherie's apartment. Possibly, I think, given Cherie's colourful past, it comes complete with a life-size stone circle and a set of bongs carved from parsnips.

'It's the best place in the world and you're going to love it,' Lizzie says. I'm not sure if I should be upset that she's so keen to get rid of me, but understand a little better when she adds: 'And, you know, I'll be able to stay with you sometimes. Away from irritating brothers and mums who try and make me eat broccoli. And . . . well, it's right by Josh's house, and . . . '

'She gets the picture,' interrupts Laura, giving Lizzie a shut-your-trap-little-miss look. It works, and Lizzie is immediately silent. Josh is the boyfriend, in case you wondered.

Laura turns to me and smiles, her eyes amused at what must be a pretty befuddled expression on my face.

'So, I've come all this way to see you guys and you're kicking me out already?' I say, half-joking.

'Not at all. You're more than welcome to stay in Hyacinth, of course you are. But . . . well, the offer is there. Cherie is finally — finally! — ready to admit defeat and stay with Frank, at least until the night before the wedding, and she offered. Said she didn't want her little Moroccan boudoir to feel all neglected.'

I grin at that description. It does sound brilliant. Straight away I can picture it: a little attic hideaway, all silk cushions and joss sticks and bowls of figs . . .

'I thought,' says Laura, walking through to the kitchen, dodging low-flying angels as she goes, 'that it might be nice. I know you're going to love it here, but I know you'll love it even more if you have your own space.'

I look around, at the tree and the streamers and the plastic holly and the big, battered sofa that's covered in floral fabric and placed strategically in front of the TV. I imagine us all, crammed in here, sharing this space, breathing this air, inhaling this tinsel, being force-fed sickly festive movies about angels' wings and miracles, while I slowly die inside.

If I have my own space, at least I can watch *Bad Santa* without worrying that it's too rude for the kids to see. If I have my own space, I can declare war on Christmas. If I have my own space, I can stretch out and walk round in my knickers and not bother washing the dishes until I'm good and ready.

If I have my own space, I can stay just about in control — surely the greatest Christmas gift of all?

'You're right,' I say, nodding. 'I would love that.'

'Good,' she replies, opening the oven and pulling out a huge, steaming pizza. 'But tonight, you're stuck with us — and guess what? We've got *Elf* on DVD . . .'

5

I am being crushed. I cannot breathe. I am gulping for my last ever lungful of oxygen before I depart this earth.

Then, suddenly, it is over — and I am free. Free from the powerful embrace of Cherie Moon, proprietor of the Comfort Food Café; owner of the Rockery, and proud purveyor of the most punishing hugs in Britain.

It is the morning after my arrival in Dorset and I am exhausted. This is a completely normal state of affairs for me in the morning. No matter how physically tired I am, my brain refuses to switch off, and I spend at least two hours every night lying awake telling myself I'm being stupid.

Telling myself to just relax. Telling myself that I need to rest, to set aside my worries, to allow my busy mind to be at peace. Counting sheep, imagining Gerard Butler naked, spending my fictional lottery winnings, anything at all other than lie there awake, worrying about the very fact that I am still awake.

But if you've ever suffered from insomnia, you'll know it's not that easy. The minutes turn into hours and the hours feel like days, and soon you start to yearn for the first sight of dawn creeping through the curtains. Then you can finally give up on your pathetic efforts and get out of bed, crawling from the duvet, grey and haggard, limping down the stairs to seek coffee like Gollum searching for his ring.

This morning, when I limped down the stairs, it was made even worse by the fact that I was in a strange place, kept banging my head on dangling angels and reindeers and had to sip my coffee while being mocked by the world's biggest Christmas tree.

By the time the others finally started to straggle back into consciousness, I'd been up for two hours, fiddling with my laptop and pretending to work.

I'm a freelance designer, which sounds a lot cooler that it is. I'm not coming up with cutting edge bathroom storage devices for Ikea, or creating the latest catwalk looks for Paris — I'm usually trying to produce bright, clear and attractive marketing materials for housing associations, charities and hospitals.

You know the kind of thing — that leaflet that tells you what to do if you can't pay your rent on time; or what services the Patient Liaison Panel provides, or how doing a charity hike across the Pennines can help people with cancer. One day, I might even get to throw caution to the wind and indulge in something like a holiday brochure or a theatre programme, who knows?

What it lacks in excitement it makes up for in flexibility. I get to be my own manager, don't always have to work in an office full of people I don't like, and usually avoid the routine of pointless meetings and bitching sessions by the water fountain. Plus I get to be creative, in however limited a way.

It also means that I get to come away and stay

in Dorset for a month without worrying about getting my leave signed off by a control-freak boss — because I am my very own control-freak boss. I've brought a few projects with me, but am not too worried about them — at this time of year, I've noticed, pretty much everyone goes quiet. Everyone becomes unofficially focused on the festive season rather than work, and projects, deadlines and delivery dates sneakily get pushed back to the New Year.

It usually drives me nuts — but this year? Well, I'm down with it.

I'm also down with being here, in the famous Comfort Food Café, now that Cherie has finally released me from her death grip and my face is no longer squished into her humungous chest.

We drove over here together and Lizzie, Nate and Laura were all three completely pipping with excitement about it. I have to admit, there was some pressure — the pressure of their obvious love for the place; the pressure of their anticipation that I'd totally share their love; the pressure to be as gah gah about the café as they are.

Me? I'm not especially good with pressure. With doing what's expected of me, or acting appropriately, or basically doing what I know I should be doing. I have a contrary streak bigger than Kim Kardashian's arse, and it sometimes gets in the way of what should be perfectly normal, pleasant situations.

So I was borderline anxious as we made the trek up the hill, pausing to admire the views on the way. The views, I have to say, did not disappoint in any way. Even without the sunshine, they are stunning — red and brown cliff faces sinking down onto golden sand; churning grey and white waves splashing onto the beach, the distant outline of the coast as it curves into Devon. Beautiful, even to a cynical old city girl like myself. I can imagine it all coated in snow, if the snow ever grows a pair of balls and gets to the sticking point. It's going to be beautiful.

I paused to take a few pictures, even though my niece was literally pulling me up the path by the hood of my fleece, half-strangling me in her eagerness to reach the café.

When we finally got there — because, of course, after that, I had to insist on stopping every few seconds to take more pictures, just to childishly assert my independence — I was slightly out of puff, and slightly wary about what I was going to find at the summit.

We walked beneath the pretty wrought-iron sign that announced we'd reached our destination, and out into the Garden at the Edge of the World. Or at least the garden on top of a very steep hill, overlooking a pretty dramatic coastline.

The ground of the café garden is uneven, with picnic-style tables and benches dotted around on the slopes. I can imagine it's packed out here in the summer, but this morning it was deserted, the faded grass and the wooden table tops dusted with frost, glistening in the pale sunlight.

I saw a few upright patio heaters nearer to the main café building, standing between more tables and chairs, and rows of fairy lights draped along the roof. A gazebo has been set up, which I know from Laura's updates has been approved as a 'licensed garden structure', which will allow weddings to take place. Specifically, Frank and Cherie's wedding. They got together officially on the night of his eightieth, and have moved fast — but I suppose at their age, you might as well.

It's all incredibly pretty, and not a big stretch to picture this place lit up and luminous, with groups of friends huddled beneath the heaters, mittened hands wrapped around steaming glasses of warm mulled wine. All chattering and laughing and bursting into spontaneous renditions of 'Jingle Bells' while they admire each other's Christmas jumpers.

That was way too festive an image for my liking, so I shook it off, and instead followed the troops into the café. The building itself was low and sprawling, and looked as though it was perched right on the cliff's edge.

Lizzie pretty much barrelled her way into the place, so confident and sure of her place in this world, and I had a moment of such fierce pride that I wanted to go and hug her and tell her I loved her right there and then. She's gorgeous, my lovely niece — blonde hair and big green eyes and a borderline Goth approach to eyeliner. She always was gorgeous, but now she's happy again, it shows even more.

I know Laura had been starting to fret about Lizzie not eating enough, and I'd started to fret about her turning out to be more like me, which I wouldn't wish on any parent.

Her dad's death knocked her for six, and Laura's ensuing emotional collapse knocked us all for about a thousand. Seeing her like this — spry and bolshy and carefree — is an absolute balm for the soul.

I follow her in, suddenly swamped with the kind of glorious warmth that makes you realise exactly how cold you've been. It was as though I hadn't even noticed my shaking hands and chattering teeth until I walked through that door, and was wrapped up in the atmospheric equivalent of a fluffy blanket embroidered with pastel-coloured kittens.

Laura, I suspect, would have seen that as some kind of analogy for the café as a whole; a place you go to heal without even knowing you're wounded. Sometimes I think she attributes it with almost supernatural powers. Me? I'm a bit more cynical than her. Always have been, most likely always will be.

But . . . I have to say, that hug from Cherie was a classic. I'm so tired, if she'd held on to me for a few more moments, I might actually have just snuggled up in her bosom and gone to sleep, like a snoozy rabbit.

'My, my! I can't believe there are two of you!' she says, pulling back and looking me up and down. I return the favour and realise that Cherie Moon in the flesh is even more impressive than the Cherie Moon I'd seen in photos.

She's tall — very tall — and big. Not fat exactly, but large and solid, built like the kind of woman who could run empires and carry milk buckets and colonise vast continents.

I know she's in her early seventies, but she looks timeless, her skin tanned and weathered, her wrinkles worn without any attempt at hiding them. Her hair is long, brown and grey, and slung over her shoulder in a fat plait. She's wearing an apron that says 'I'm Sexy And I Know It', and she smells so good. Of vanilla and sugar and freshly baked deliciousness. I would ask her if she could adopt me, if it wouldn't upset my biological parents.

'Yep,' I say, smiling, because it's impossible to do anything else. 'Two of us. Our parents were very, very lucky people.'

'That they were . . . though you look like you need a bit more flesh on your bones, my love. A few weeks here will sort that out — get a bit of your Laura's home-made cooking down you!'

I see Laura at her side, also smiling, so relaxed, and think for the millionth time how fantastic it is that she made this brave move. That she ignored all the doubters, ignored our parents, ignored every sensible piece of advice she got and did the Crazy Thing. Because sometimes the Crazy Thing is exactly what your life needs.

And looking around the Comfort Food Café, I see a very healthy dose of crazy — bookcases crammed with paperbacks and board games, insane mobiles made from random objects dangling from the ceiling, plastic fish, framed photos, rowing oars, life rings, fishing nets, posters with pithy messages, giant fossils. It's like an eccentric Victorian collector's dream.

There are also, I see, the beginnings of Christmas decorations starting to appear, and

49

Cherie has an enormous cardboard box at her feet that has sparkly things oozing out of it. I hope she doesn't expect me to be streamer girl. I don't want to be adopted quite that much.

'Can we take Aunt Becca up to the flat, Cherie?' asks Lizzie, still fizzing in anticipation. Nate, I notice, has taken his traditionally more laid-back approach, has lobbed his padded jacket onto a table and is already sniffing around the cake counter eyeing up the world's largest Victoria sponge.

'Course we can, sweetie,' replies Cherie, wiping her hands down on her apron and giving Lizzie's hair a quick pat. It is testament to their relationship that Lizzie doesn't immediately punch her in the throat.

'Come on, Becca,' she says to me. 'Let me show you my des res. Sad to leave it, I am, but . . . well, life changes, doesn't it? I'm heading off to live in sin with Frank — shocking at my age! At least 'til we make it legal in a few weeks' time . . . Laura, can you keep an eye on the place?'

Laura looks around at the completely empty café.

'I'm not sure I can cope with the rush, Cherie,' she replies, giving her a wink.

'Less of your cheek, madam — you know how it can get. One minute it's deserted, the next there's a coach party in, all wanting scrambled eggs and mochas . . . '

'I know. I've got a few ideas I want to try anyway, for the Christmas menu. I've been experimenting with cranberry ice cream, but even Midgebo wouldn't touch it, it was that bad.'

50

We all pull a shocked face. If something tastes so awful that a Labrador won't gobble it up, it must have been very special indeed.

I follow Cherie through the bright, shiny kitchen, noticing the very slight hitch in her stride that is the only hint of the hip replacement she had a few months ago. We continue up a very narrow flight of stairs, which I see are now decorated with fluorescent strips.

'Frank's idea of health and safety,' she says over her shoulder. 'After I had my fall. I told him I just see them as go-faster stripes, but he will have his jokes . . . might come in handy if you're ever trying to get back up here after a few tipples though, eh?'

I see that my reputation has preceded me and know that Laura has undoubtedly painted me as a good-time girl not to be trusted with the sherry bottle. Little do they know.

We emerge up into what I can only describe as a very tiny slice of paradise. It's not the brightest of days outside, but what sunlight there is is streaming through the attic windows, bathing the whole place in yellow stripes. There is one big room, which contains pretty much everything I could ever need.

There's a bed, a TV, a squishy-looking sofa and a small kitchen area off in one corner. The walls are decorated with framed posters from classic rock albums, like the velvet Underground and The Doors and The Who, and one of the sloping eaves is covered with a beautiful, exotic-looking red fabric that looks like Cherie haggled for it at a car-boot sale in Marrakesh.

There's a vast collection of vinyl, which Lizzie immediately gravitates toward and various foreign-looking objects that again don't seem to have been picked up at the local Ikea. There's a hint of incense in the air — or possibly something stronger, if Laura's description of Cherie's smoking habits are to be believed — and an entire book-case filled with pictures of the lady herself, over the years.

I stroll over and pick one up; it's in that fuzzy technicolour that was once considered glorious, and now looks faded and dated — the kind my mum and dad have in their photo album, from the pre-digital age.

I see Cherie, a good forty years younger, still tall and imposing, but a lot more lithe, barefoot and wearing a bikini. She's lying at the side of a pool with a man with a lot of long, black hair and furry sideburns. They look impossibly glamorous, poster children for the seventies.

'That's me and my Wally,' she says, standing next to me and smiling at the memory. 'St Tropez. Some kind of showbiz event, it was. Lots of bands there. You couldn't move for the TVs that'd got thrown out the windows.'

I snort, suspecting she is joking but not quite sure. It does look like the kind of place you'd see Janis Joplin sipping a margarita. I think, with Cherie, that the mystery adds to the fun — I've been told that half the village still thinks she was Jimi Hendrix's secret girlfriend.

'You look really happy,' I reply, stroking the glass clear of a speck of dust and standing it back up again.

'That's 'cause we were, my love. We had a great life together, we did — and now it looks like I've been lucky enough to find someone who'll put up with me second time round. Just like your Laura has.'

'That is lucky,' I say, gazing at the rest of the pictures — a long, rich life captured in film. 'I'm still waiting to find the first.'

I'm not really sure why I say such a thing, and I'm certainly not sure why I say it with the melancholy tinge I hear lacing my own words as they leave my mouth. I've always been happy being a lone wolf. At least that's what I tell myself when I'm howling at the moon.

'Well who knows, eh?' answers Cherie, giving me a nudge so hard I take several steps to the side and almost collide with a wooden hat stand that's topped with a carved dragon's head. 'Maybe you'll find him here. Stranger things have happened at sea.'

I automatically look out of the windows and down to the coast, where the sea is churning up against the sand.

Somehow, I doubt there is anything stranger out there than me.

6

Matt is, as promised, every bit the young Harrison Ford. He's tall, on the brawny side, and has floppy chestnut brown hair that needs a trim. He's quiet, softly spoken, and seems to truly come alive when he's talking to Laura.

My sister, sitting next to him at the big table, surrounded by friends and her new family, looks just as vibrant. She and Matt are chatting to other people, but I can tell by the way they're sitting that beneath that table, their legs are crushed up against each other's. Like they can't bear to break contact.

I'm struck again by how gloriously different she is now. This time last year, she was functioning, but still crippled by grief at David's loss. Those first Christmases without him were pure torture, for everyone involved.

The kids got the best and brightest presents out there, simply because she blew a small chunk of her insurance money on them, in an attempt to make up for the life she knew they were lacking. I remember her nibbling at a few mouthfuls of her turkey, the kids quiet and withdrawn, my parents desperate to find a way to reach her.

They couldn't. All we could do was play along with the fake smiles and the charade of familial unity she chose to present to us, and help out with the kids as much as we could. The real

Laura, the one that was suffering, was buried beneath the school runs and the domestic-goddess cooking and the relentless walking of an old, fat dog.

Now, though, Matt had managed the impossible — he'd reached her. They all had, all of these people, here, gathered around this table, in this café. Closed to the public now, open just to us, celebrating something odd — my arrival in Budbury. The prodigal sister, joining in the feast.

Cherie is at the head of the table, sipping her wine and laughing joyfully at something Frank has just whispered to her. Frank himself — always known as Farmer Frank to me — is also grinning, his weather-worn face a road map of lines and experience, his blue eyes shining almost as brightly as the silver of his hair. His grandson, Luke, is with him — an eighteen-year-old sunshine kid who grew up in Australia, but is staying with him for a while, doing work experience with Matt on his gap year.

There's the Scrumpy Jones collective, as they're nicknamed. Joe, the dad, lean and dark and speaking with a Dorset accent so thick I can barely understand him. Joe runs the Cider Cave, and his wife, Joanne, is a frosted piece of eighties hair who looks unhappy to be out in company. Their son, Josh, is Lizzie's boyfriend — a lanky beanpole of a sixteen-year-old, wearing a beanie hat and a checked shirt that looks like it needs a wash.

Lizzie is by his side, doing something with her phone, occasionally flashing him a smile that tells me he is the absolute centre of her entire world. Scary, that look — I used it once before, myself, when I wasn't much older than her. When a boy like Josh was the centre of my entire world too. He's a manager at the local Aldi now, Shaun, and I sometimes bump into him when I'm shopping.

We both pretend we haven't seen each other — him bustling away to make an announcement at the check-out, me taking a sudden interest in the sweet potatoes. Even after all these years, all this *life*, it still cuts. Still stirs up thoughts and feelings that I know will derail me if I let them. I can only hope that Lizzie has a happier ending than I did, and be there for her if she doesn't.

Willow, the pink-haired supermodel from the future who works at the café, is sitting with Nate. She has tattoos and piercings and generally looks like a handful of trouble. I'm pretty sure we'll get on well. The two of them are playing noughts and crosses, and the bet seems to be for who loads the dishwasher once our feast is over.

Next to me is Edie May. I can't put into words how much I already love Edie May. She is ninety years old and looks like a naughty imp. Her grey hair is permed and cut close to her tiny head.

Every one of these people already feels familiar to me through Lizzie's summer photos and my conversations with Laura. I know that each of them has a very special comfort food that the café provides — for Frank, it's the burned bacon butties his late wife used to serve up for him. For Joe, it's the almond biscotti that remind him of his childhood holidays with family in Italy.

For Edie, it's an extra portion of whatever's going — to be taken back to her tiny house in the village, as a treat for the fiancé who was killed in the war. To Edie, though, he's still real — and who am I to disagree?

'You're not eating much of your lasagne, my love,' she says, pointing at my plate. She's right. I've been squishing it around for a while, hoping nobody will notice. It's a great lasagne. Laura made it, so of course it is. But I'm feeling a little . . . well, trapped. I'm used to my own company. To dinners for one in front of the TV. To doing whatever the hell I like.

Here, I am surrounded by people who expect . . . well, I have no idea what they expect. They clearly all love and adore Laura and are willing to love and adore me by default. The problem is, I am nowhere near as lovable as my sister, and am sure to say or do something inappropriate that proves it before very long.

'I ate earlier, Edie,' I reply, meeting wise old eyes that are submerged in a layer of lines and creases. 'In fact I've been eating all day. From the moment I got here, I seem to have been presented with nothing but food . . . '

'Well, that's the nature of the beast, my dear. It's how those ladies over there — your sister, Cherie — show that they care about us, isn't it? If they were florists, we'd all be draped in roses, wouldn't we? Anyway. Pudding's coming now. At least you saved a space, eh?'

She gives me a little wink and I automatically wink back. She winks again and I return it. We sit there, twitching at each other, for a good minute or so, until we both dissolve into laughter at how silly we're being. If this is what being in your nineties is like, it might be worth hanging around for.

I feel a soft, wet touch on my ankle and realise that the dog is under the table. At least I hope he is. Midgebo is a delightful bringer of chaos — not yet one, but huge, all shiny black fur and typical Labrador energy. I sneak a chunk of bread down by my side and he almost takes my hand off. He has yet to develop table manners, it seems, and is probably having a fine old time under there, minesweeping.

Willow's dog — a Border Terrier called Bella Swan — is tucked away in her basket in the corner of the room, far too classy to get involved in such degrading shenanigans.

Willow herself is now clearing the table, with Nate and Lizzie's help, as Cherie emerges from the kitchen with an enormous trifle. I see that it is made with chocolate custard, and understand immediately that Laura has made it just for me. It was always my favourite when I was growing up. I used to make it with packets of Angel Delight and eat a whole bowl to myself, locked in the airing cupboard, emerging covered in gunk and holding a sore tummy. I was a delightful child.

This is a posher version, but essentially the same. Comfort food, of course.

Cherie plonks it down on the table and starts to scoop huge portions out into glass bowls. There is low music playing in the background — something a tiny bit jazzy — and everyone is chattering away among themselves. They've all been drinking for some time now, at least the adults have, and there is a lot of loud, raucous laughter.

The lighting is low, and the views out of the patio windows down to the bay are amazing. It is, I think, pretty much perfect. I can see why Laura never wanted to leave.

On cue, she walks over, sitting on the other side of me at the table, delivering a vast acreage of trifle and a bottle of Prosecco.

'You okay?' she asks, a slight frown on her face.

'Of course I am,' I reply. 'I don't care what the scientists say. That alien abduction last week did me no harm at all.'

'Oh,' she replies, eyes widening. 'I didn't realise you'd been abducted by aliens again. I hope they didn't get anal on you?'

'No. It was all very civilised. They just wanted me to design them a new poster for their Martian Cup football tournament.'

'That's all right, then. Drink?'

She tilts the bottle towards my glass, but I quickly put my hand over it. Laura, of course, has no idea that I don't drink any more. That I don't smoke any more. That I don't indulge in any slightly illegal pharmaceuticals any more. It was a decision I made the day David died, but one I kept very quiet.

Partly, I just didn't want to set myself up to fail, to disappoint people I'd disappointed so many times before. Partly, she was simply too lost in her own wilderness to notice me trying to navigate mine.

She looks momentarily confused, but tops her own glass up anyway. That's good. She's a heck of a lot of fun when she's drunk, my sister. We can anticipate dancing on the tabletops before long.

'So, what do you think?' she asks, glancing around at her gathered friends. Nate has gone over to sit with Bella Swan, who is regally ignoring him, and Midgebo is prancing around them both, sniffing and snorting and wagging his tail so fast it's just a shady blur.

'I think you're happy. And that makes me happy.'

She nods and quietly sips her wine.

'Sometimes,' she says, after a few beats of silence, 'I think maybe I'm too happy. I'm here, with a new life. A new man. Even a new dog, for goodness' sake. And I feel . . . guilty. Sad that David's not here, ashamed that occasionally, I go a whole morning without thinking about him . . . '

'Hmm . . . did you ever meet David?' I ask, which is obviously a stupid question as she had two kids with him. 'Because the David I knew wouldn't have wanted anything else. The David I knew would be wishing you well, cheering you on, proud of you. I've not seen Lizzie and Nate so happy for years. I've not seen you like this for just as long. Moving on doesn't mean you're leaving him behind.'

'I know . . . ' she replies, and I see a sheen of tears in her green eyes. 'You're right, the logical part of me gets that. I'm so lucky, to have found this place. These people. But hey, we're not always logical, are we?'

'I for one pride myself on never being logical. It's one of my most endearing qualities, as you know. But even my screwed-up view of life doesn't allow you to feel guilty about this — about living. So put a sock in it and have another drink.'

She laughs and does exactly that. I make the most of the pause to shove a huge spoonful of trifle in my mouth and she makes the most of that to start talking again.

'So. On a totally different subject — Sam will be getting here later. He's been in London for a week, doing Jurassic Coast workshops with kids in museums and libraries — drove off into the sunset with a big van of fossils . . . anyway, I can't wait for you to meet him.'

She raises her eyebrows and does a kind of Benny Hill face, suggesting that by the word 'meet', she actually means 'shag the arse off'. I can understand why she thinks this is likely. I have, to put it politely, played the field in my time.

It must all have looked like great fun to her. She was busy changing nappies and I was picking up Brazilian exchange students in nightclubs. And for a while, it was fun. Until . . . well, until it wasn't. Until it started to make me feel even lonelier than being on my own. Until the emptiness of it started to bite, and I'd find myself in tears, waking up with yet another piece of divine manhood whose name I didn't know.

What can I say? It wasn't pretty. And yet

61

another part of my life that is now well and truly over.

Sam — known as Surfer Sam — is another one of her Budbury friends. Lizzie sent me loads of pictures of him over the summer, sun-dappled and hot on his bodyboard, all shaggy blonde hair and dimples and long, lean muscles. Laura was blatantly pimping him out, and he didn't seem to mind. I played along and made all the right appreciative noises — which was fine when I was safely tucked away in Manchester. Now I'm here, I need to nip it in the bud before she goes all Jane Austen's *Emma* on our asses.

I slurp down the last bit of trifle, which is, incidentally, delicious, and say: 'Don't get any ideas, sis. You should know I'm on a diet.'

'It's hard to take that statement seriously when you have chocolate custard smeared all over your face,' she replies, passing me a napkin so I can wipe it off.

'I mean a sex diet. Gorgeous as your Surfer Sam might be, bonking is not on the menu — so stop trying to ram him down my throat. As it were.'

She pauses, inspects my face, and uses another napkin to dab at the bit I've missed. Sometimes she is so much like my mother I could happily throttle her. I suppose I'm lucky she didn't spit on it first.

'Well, we'll see, won't we? I've never known you to stick to any kind of diet before for the whole of your life. And you've not even met him yet. He might sweep you off your feet. That kind of thing can happen here. And at Christmas.'

She looks so convinced of all of this — so sure that she understands me and what I need — that I feel like a complete heel for keeping things from her. Now she's healthier, perhaps I should be more honest. That, though, will take some thought — and some solitude. For now, I need to get through the night.

'I applaud your faith in miracles, Laura, I really do,' I say. 'But no. Just no. And now . . . well, I'm just nipping outside for a bit, all right?'

'Fag break?' she asks.

'No, I just need to shoot up a bit of heroin, okay? And I'm taking one of these spoons.'

I grab a spoon — which is downright silly, as it too is coated in chocolate custard — and make for the door.

Once I'm outside, I feel free. Like I can breathe again. I also feel, it has to be noted, bloody freezing. The snow that has been floating around off and on all day has lowered the temperature right down, and I'm wearing skinny jeans and a blouse. I've left my sweater over the back of the chair, and my skin immediately puckers up with the cold as I lick the chocolate off the spoon and shove it into my pocket.

Still, I needed the break. I glance down at the bay, at the moonlight reflecting off the waves, at the wide open space and the completely deserted beach, and it calms me down. I love my sister, and her kids, and I genuinely like everyone I've met in Budbury so far. But there just comes a point where I need to suck in oxygen alone.

I've been this way since being a small child

and it's unlikely to change. Laura's always been more sociable than me. More friendly. More likable, basically. I always get to a stage where no matter how much I'm enjoying myself, I make a run for it — whether that's for the garden outside a clifftop café or jumping into a black cab and leaving my friends in a busy bar in Manchester.

For a moment, I wish I was still a smoker. That was always a fabulous reason to nip out for a minute — but the downside of lung cancer and COPD just doesn't seem to be worth it.

Instead, I pause for a second, bathed in the lights shining from inside the café, listening to the chatter and the music and the laughter and cursing myself for not being able to be part of that world. Then I go through one of my more insane rituals — I pull a fictional cigarette packet from my jeans pocket, followed by my fictional cigarette lighter. A really nice Zippo, because if you're going to have a fictional lighter, it might as well be a good one.

I extract a fictional Marlborough Light from the pack and put it in my mouth. I spark up the lighter and take my first glorious puff. And there I stand, pretending I'm smoking, like the loon that I am.

I have been doing this for a few seconds when I hear the footsteps. Boots crunching on frosty grass, walking towards me from the darkened corner of the building. I adopt my Manchester street stance and wonder if I should have a key grasped between my knuckles like my mother always taught me.

I look cautiously at the figure that's approaching. Male. Tall. Blonde. Pretty damn gorgeous. And very obviously amused.

'Hey,' he says, coming to a halt in front of me. 'Would you mind if I had one of your imaginary cigarettes?'

Oh good. Not a serial killer, but a witness to behaviour I'd much rather remain unwitnessed.

'I'm not sure,' I reply, my voice catching up with my brain. 'Just let me check how many I've got left.'

I look in the imaginary packet and nod, pulling one out for him.

Sam — and I know it is him. I recognise him from the photos — graciously accepts it, pops it in his mouth and waits for me to light it for him.

He takes a long, exaggerated drag, and I have to laugh. Clearly he's as bonkers as I am.

'I thought I'd just about given up as well . . . ' he says, his tone a perfect mix of pleasure and disappointment.

He drops the cigarette-that-doesn't-exist and pretends to grind it out with his big, muddy boot.

'I'm Sam,' he says, offering a hand to shake. 'And I'm guessing you must be Becca.'

He smiles and it is dazzling. He has a blissfully lovely Irish accent, his blue eyes are bright and mischievous, and his fingers around mine are strong and welcomingly warm. Straight away I feel a spark between us, brighter than the flame from my imaginary Zippo.

Oh shit, I think, as I eventually follow him back into the café. That kind of spark doesn't bode well for me at all.

Neither does the fact that the table is being cleared, and what looks like a very spirited — and by that I mean drunk — game of charades is in progress. I guess you have to make your own fun when you live in the middle of nowhere.

I settle back down in my chair, aware of the fact that Sam is going around the room getting hugs from everyone, and hoping he doesn't come and sit next to me. I need time to calm down after that spark-y thing.

Approximately two minutes later, of course, he sits down at my side. He's shed the winter jacket and the beanie hat, and beneath he is wearing a form-fitting long-sleeved T-shirt with Japanese writing on it. It probably translates as 'Danger-ously Hot Dude'.

He gives me a cheeky wink, and I can't help but smile back at him. He's one of those people who is so infectiously happy that you'd have to work very hard not to go along with it.

'This,' he says, leaning towards me and whispering, 'is what passes for a wild night out round here. Be prepared to be blown away.'

'I already am,' I reply, pointing at Cherie, who is currently miming what appears to be a crazed serial killer repeatedly attacking a dwarf. She has an imaginary weapon in her hand, possibly a sword or an axe or an especially sharp pencil, and is slashing away at thin air with it. People are randomly shouting out the names of films, like *Psycho* and *The Shining*, and each time she shakes her head in frustration.

She then grabs her hair in one hand, and holds it up in the air until it's in one thick strand pointing skywards. The whole thing is mystifying and making me laugh so much my chair is rattling.

Eventually, after breaking down the little words and doing some kind of Indian-warrior hand-on-mouth movement, Frank finally gets it: *The Last of the Mohicans*. Of course. Why didn't we get that?

Sam nudges me, and I see that he is also cracking up. We are the only truly sober people here, which somehow makes it all even funnier.

Laura is up next, and I see her face crease into a grimace as she picks her crumpled bit of paper from the tobacco box where they're stored. We've played this game more times than I care to remember, and suspect I will have a head start on everyone else, knowing how her mind works.

Little do I know. She starts making a wand-waving gesture and segues neatly into miming a person hanging from a noose. That is literally all it takes before Matt shouts out: '*Harry Potter and the Deathly Hallows*!' Ok, she was miming 'gallows', but I get it.

She pauses, gives him a radiant smile, and holds up two fingers.

'Part 2!' he adds, and everyone bursts into applause. She runs over to him and sits on his knee, and I see that he immediately wraps his arms around her. They are so good together, and I feel a thrill of vicarious pleasure shoot through me. It's so well deserved.

One by one, pretty much everyone takes a

turn, and I am in hysterics throughout. What makes sense to an inebriated person rarely makes sense to a sober one, and the end result is a mishmash of flailing arms and legs, strange shapes, face-pulling and in Scrumpy Joe's case, leaping up and down repeatedly on the spot to successfully act out *21 Jump Street*.

Pretty much my favourite of the night is Edie May, who might be ninety but still has the sense of humour of a nineteen-year-old. She takes those small, careful old-lady steps up to the front of the room, puts her tiny wrinkled hands on her hips, and proceeds to do the most disgustingly suggestive bump and grind I've ever seen. At least from someone old enough to be my great grandma.

I am laughing so hard I can barely breathe, and when I look over at him, I see that Sam has tears streaming down his face and is holding his sides.

Eventually, after a good couple of minutes of Edie's frankly horrifying naughtiness, the whole room echoing with laughter, Cherie shouts: '*Dirty Dancing*! For God's sake, Edie, please, stop!'

I lean back in my chair and feel in need of an oxygen mask, I've been laughing so hard. Sam wipes the tears from his eyes and says: 'I will never watch that movie again.'

'Well,' I reply, finally able to breathe, 'you know what they say. Nobody puts Edie in a corner.'

By that stage, it's only me and Sam left to take a turn. Laura calls my name and I get to my feet, still shaking from too much giggling. I take my paper and see written on it 'Wuthering Heights'. This, I decide, is a tricky one. There are no little words. No clear mime for Wuthering. I could maybe gesture up to the ceiling for Heights, but it would be a while before anyone got that.

Instead — bearing in mind most of these people are hammered and really won't remember tomorrow — I decide to go full-on Kate Bush. I grab a tablecloth as a prop and use it like a cape, wafting it around me as I dance and leap and look as balletic as I possibly can. There is a lot of laughter, which I completely understand, and Lizzie randomly cries out: 'Black Swan — the Magic Mushroom Edition!', which makes everyone hoot even more.

I do some swirls and spins and then go for a high leg kick, which isn't as easy as it sounds in skinny jeans. One of my shoes flies off and clonks Frank on the side of the head. I don't break character, but I do mouth a quick 'sorry' as I flutter around the room.

By the time I build up to my finale, doing the bit where Kate mimes a window, I am convinced that all is lost — until Sam stands up and yells: 'I know! *Wuthering Heights*!'

I sigh in relief and make that odd nose gesture that for some reason means you've got it in charades. Everyone applauds and I take a bow before returning to my seat, where I collapse in a sweaty and way-too-out-of-puff heap. God, that Kate Bush must have been fit.

'That was brilliant,' he says, patting me on the thigh. 'A live re-enactment of one of the most erotic memories of my childhood.'

I'm not quite sure how to reply to this and also don't have much breath left, so it's a good thing that Laura finally calls out his name.

He reads his paper and walks to centre stage. He tells us all it is four words and a film, then bends over and makes a blowing gesture with his hands that to me instantly says 'this is a man in the throes of a huge fart attack.'

That's all it takes.

'*Gone With The Wind!*' I shout, while everyone else is still looking confused. He jumps up straight and grins at me across the room.

More applause, as he makes his way back to me. Laura puts some music on, and a few of them start dancing. I am still worn out from Heathcliffing my way through my routine and stay put.

'So,' says Sam, sitting so close I can feel his jean-clad thighs touching mine. 'Was that just as erotic for you?'

I burst out laughing, which is obviously what he intended, but don't answer. I'm a bit worried about what I might say, and I'm also aware that we are under surveillance. Laura is studying me from across the room, a hopeful smile on her face.

I know what she's thinking. That I get him, and he gets me.

The only thing she doesn't get, of course, is the fact that I don't want anybody to get me right now — because I'm not all that worth having.

7

We are sitting in the snug of a pub known affectionately — apparently — as the Blue-Arse Fly. This is, I think, because its actual name is the Blue Bottle, and the swinging wooden sign outside it bears a painted version of an olde-worlde-looking glass jar in a dazzling shade of cerulean.

It's almost a week since I arrived in Budbury and I am settling slightly better into life here. That's partly because everyone else has been busy — Lizzie and Nate back in school, Laura and Cherie cooking up wedding plans, Willow running the café without them.

This has come as a slight relief, and I have enjoyed the last few days — strolling on the beach with Midgebo, collecting interesting-looking sticks and rocks that I must remember to put back; getting to know a few more of the locals, and taking tea with Edie May.

I've done some work, taken a lot of photos, eaten enough to sink a juggernaut and walked for miles and miles and miles. The weather has been cold and clear and crisp, and the views out over the sea have been almost life-changing in their beauty.

I've watched a box set of *Mad Men* that I found in the games room at the Rockery; practised my Betty Draper accent as a result; listened to a lot of Cherie's vinyl and spoken to

71

my parents a couple of times.

I've been lazily busy doing nothing, and it's been very pleasant.

What I've not been doing, though, is engaging with the casual flirtation that Surfer Sam has been offering up on a saucy plate. At least I've been trying not to — it goes against all instincts, if I'm honest. Sam is a coastal ranger, and most of his work is outdoors — most of it, in fact, seems to happen in and around the exact location of the cafe. I see him driving around in his jeep, wearing his cargo pants and thick green fleece, and then pretend I haven't seen him at all.

So far he's joined me for a walk on the beach — pointing out fascinating geological features as we went, in an accent that made even that sound sexy — and asked me out for a drink approximately eight times. I've always said no, because a) I don't drink, and b) I am on a sex diet. Not that I used those exact words.

He's presented me with a 'perfectly formed ammonite', adding 'there's more where that came from,' and a cheeky wink; he's shared his coffee flask with me down on the beach and he's smoked several more imaginary ciggies.

I know — from the general way the man behaves and from what Laura has told me — that none of this is to be taken too seriously. He's an attractive and naturally flirtatious creature. He flexes his charm muscles on all the ladies in the café, and takes the resulting hoots of derision from Cherie and Willow with great humour. He's grown up surrounded by women

— a mother and a huge gaggle of sisters back in Dublin — and quite clearly likes them.

The problem doesn't lie with him. It lies with me. I made this stupid rule for myself — no more one-night stands — and now I have to live with it. So far, it's been easy. Maybe I just haven't met anybody tempting in Manchester for a while. Maybe, if I'm being unkind to myself, I've simply crossed all the available men there off my 'been there, done that' list.

Sam, however, is a slightly different proposition. He's funny and kind and gorgeous and, well, if I'm blunt, looks like he'd be a good shag. I am tempted, and for me, that's not a good sign. I've worked stupidly hard at cleaning my life up and it's been a battle I've fought alone. I've not joined support groups or been to the GP or even enlisted the help of my family.

I quit everything, cold turkey, the day I went with Laura and Lizzie and Nate to the hospital where David was lying, hooked up to the machines that were keeping him alive. The machines that Laura had to decide to turn off. Watching her agony, watching the kids veer between tearful and confused, watching David himself — a man who had been part of my life as long as I could remember — made me realise that I needed to be strong. For myself and for them.

I was never an alcoholic. Never an addict in the proper sense of the word. I had no physical problem with stopping and always had done, periodically, just to prove to myself that I could. If I wanted to, I could go weeks without indulging — but I'd fallen into a pattern of behaviour that made all my self-destructive tendencies seem normal. It was a part of me that had become accepted — until the day I decided they were unacceptable.

I'm not expecting medals for this decision. It was my own fault I was in that mess in the first place. But somehow, they're all tied in with each other — it's as though I can do absolutely nothing in moderation, including abstinence. I am possibly doing myself a disservice, but it feels a little like if I have one cigarette, I will immediately turn into a cocaine-snorting nymphomaniac sleeping in a crack house on a bed of vodka bottles.

Same goes for one drink. Or one casual sexual encounter. So, for me, Surfer Sam is more than a cute guy with a good knack for saucy one-liners.

For me, he is a potential disaster.

Right now, the potential disaster is at the bar, with my sister, getting the drinks in. Frank and Cherie were with us earlier, but went home after a couple of pints because 'we're just old fogies'. Neither of them will be seeing seventy again, but they're both fit as fiddles and have none of the fogey about them — I suspected they were going home for some hanky panky, but didn't like to ponder it too deeply.

I am left sitting at a long, wooden table with Matt, the Hot Vet. The pub is busy and we have a spot right by a gorgeous stone fireplace. The mantelpiece is decorated with holly wreaths and every now and then I hear Christmas music wafting in from the main bar. Less than three weeks to go until the Big Day, and then it's all over for another year — thank God. Although, to be fair, it's all his fault in the first place.

Matt is, as usual, on the silent side. He's dressed up — by countryside standards — in a smart blue shirt and clean jeans. He's making his first drink last, and also, I can't help but noticing, constantly looking at his watch. As I am the designated driver for the night, I'm not sure why he's so concerned about the time. Or why he's lagging behind on the drinking front, nursing the pint of Guinness in front of him.

'Do you have somewhere else to be?' I finally ask. Matt has made my sister the happiest she's been for years, but this is the first time I have been alone with him. I fight down a sudden urge to quiz him about his prospects and ask him if his intentions are honourable.

'Ah . . . no,' he replies, pulling his cuff sharply down so it covers his watch, looking off to the side as though he has something to hide. He wouldn't make the best of poker players and I think I might have an idea of what is going on here.

'You remember in those early days, with Laura?' I ask, innocently. His face immediately breaks out into a smile, which is super-sweet. He nods, and I carry on.

'Those days before you properly got together? When Frank and Cherie were still trying to match you up, and kept trying to arrange dates?'

He is looking increasingly uncomfortable now, which confirms my suspicions. I press ahead, like Carrie Mathison interrogating a suspect in *Homeland*.

'And that time you all agreed to go out for dinner together, and then Frank and Cherie both came down with mystery illnesses at the last minute, so you two ended up alone?'

'I do remember that,' he replies, one corner of his mouth twitching into a reluctant grin. I know from my sister that that night ended up with the two of them rolling around in a wheat field, so I'm not surprised it's a happy place for him.

'Well you'll also remember that both of you were annoyed with them for setting you up. For manipulating you. For trying to back you into a corner. If that were to happen to me and Sam — say, for example, if you and Laura were to suddenly have to dash home any time soon, to deal with a Midgebo-based emergency or a made-up disaster back at Hyacinth — I'd be annoyed too. Just saying.'

I sip my Coke and narrow my eyes at him over the top of the glass. I see various emotions flicker across his face, and his expression eventually settles into one of amusement. I realise that he is trying not to laugh at me, which certainly never seemed to happen to Carrie Mathison. I must be doing this wrong.

'I can understand that,' he says, leaning back and crossing his arms over his chest in a slightly challenging way. 'But I think you're forgetting something.'

'What?' I ask.

'You're forgetting the way it ended. And the fact that Cherie and Frank were one hundred per cent right. Sometimes we just need a little nudge to understand what's good for us.'

I would love to debate this one with him, but he is spared my tirade by the arrival of my sister and Surfer Sam. Sam is also dressed up, by which I mean his cargo pants are clean and he's wearing Timberlands instead of his usual steel toe-caps. His unruly blonde hair is freshly washed and his blue eyes are sparkling over the pint glass he is holding.

Laura drops four bags of peanuts on the tabletop and places another Coke in front of me. She does not, I note, sit down, even though Sam settles himself in the corner seat, stretching his legs out in front of him so his feet snake under the table.

'I'm so sorry,' she says, looking and sounding flustered. 'But we have to go. I just had a call from Lizzie and apparently the dishwasher has flooded the kitchen ... Matt, are you still all right to drive? It's lucky you've been a slow coach on the drinking front tonight!'

I have to admit, she is a much better actress than I would have anticipated, and of course she has no way of knowing that she's already been rumbled. Matt laughs out loud and walks over to wrap his arms around her. He's so big and tall, all I can still see of her is crazy brown curls popping around his chest.

'Yep, that's really lucky, isn't it?' he says, grinning at me over her head. 'Come on. We better go home and stop the cottage from turning into Waterworld.'

'Shall I come and help?' I ask, pretending to be concerned. 'All hands to the deck?'

'Oh, no, no, don't worry!' says Laura, a bit too

quickly. 'She said it was only a small flood, nothing me and Matt can't handle. You stay here with Sam and enjoy your night.'

Matt is, by this stage, in absolute hysterics, and my sister is giving him daggers. Sam is looking mystified by the whole thing, which at least shows he wasn't in on it. I shall refrain from beating him to death with a packet of Planters purely for that reason.

'Come on, you nutter,' Matt says to Laura, leading her away by the hand. He pauses in the doorway, and gives me a little salute. I return it, grinning back at him. She is a nutter. And it's nice to see, even if it is irritating in this particular instance.

I hear them chattering away to each other as they walk to the carpark, towards Matt's truck. The truck he was allegedly leaving here overnight. I glance out of the window and see her leaning against the door of the van, creased in two she's laughing so hard. Looks like he told her.

'What's going on?' Sam asks, frowning in confusion. 'And does this mean we can eat all the bags of nuts?'

By this point I have already torn open a packet and shoved a mouthful in. I hold up my finger to gesture for him to wait for a second before I can speak. Or at least speak without being totally gross.

'They're trying to set us up,' I say finally. 'Or at least Laura is. I just can't believe she's stooped so low as to involve the dishwasher in all this.'

'Yeah. That is low,' he replies, mulling over

what I've told him, while he also eats some peanuts. I look at him and he looks at me. We stay like this for a few seconds, until he winks at me and breaks the moment. It makes me laugh out loud, it's done with such a *Carry On*-style exaggeration.

'Like what you see, little lady?' he asks.

'No. I'm just wondering how good you are at catching moving peanuts in your mouth.'

'It's one of my all-time specialist skills. Take me for a test drive, if you like.'

He leans back and angles his head into a position that suggests he has played this game before. He opens his mouth and I do an upward throw that arcs high before it drops, and he darts his face rapidly to one side so it lands perfectly.

'Wow,' I say. 'You are almost at international level there.'

'I know,' he replies, looking proud of himself. 'I could have played for Ireland. So. Laura's trying to fix us up, is she?'

'Yes. I think she's actually been trying to fix us up since the summer.'

'The photos, you mean?'

'Yeah. The ones of you parading around almost naked, strutting your stuff like you were modelling for a Coastal Ranger calendar.'

'That,' he answers, pointing at me, 'is actually a genius of an idea. We could do it for charity, with strategically placed belemnites over our man parts . . . '

'How big a belemnite?'

'That'd be telling, now, wouldn't it? So — how do you feel about this whole setting-up business?

I have to be truthful. I think it's inevitable. You and me, getting together.'

I snort a bit of Coke from my mouth as he says it, because he is trying to keep his face straight and he's failing.

'Why? You're irresistible to all women, are you?'

'Well, I'd like to say yes, but Edie gave me the knock back at her ninetieth birthday party . . . still stings.'

He clutches his hands to his heart, as though it is physically cracking at the memory, and I roll my eyes at him. He's a bit of a clown, a quality I find highly attractive in a human being.

'And Laura was never interested, either.'

'Because of Supervet?' I ask, already knowing the answer.

'Yes. Because of Supervet. They were meant for each other, those two.'

'And I'm happy for her. My sister was meant to be in love. Meant to be in a partnership. I'm not. I can barely even tolerate my own company, never mind anybody else's.'

'Well that's a pity,' he says, meeting my eyes and making me feel a little bit hot and bothered. 'I think we could have a lot of fun, don't you?'

'Possibly,' I reply, non-commitally. I see the mock-devastated look on his face, and laugh.

'Okay, probably.'

He rolls up his shirtsleeve and makes a Schwarzenegger-style pose with his arms, bulking up his biceps and raising his eyebrows in a 'well-what-do-you-think-of-these-babies?' expression.

I throw up my hands in defeat and resist the

urge to do what I know he wants me to; reach out and squeeze his muscles to see how ripped he is. I am attempting to stick to a strict 'look but don't touch' policy.

'All right. I give in. We would definitely have a lot of fun. But you wouldn't respect me in the morning.'

'That's not true,' he says quickly. 'I'd respect you even more if I got to see you naked.'

'I won't respect myself, though, you see.'

This is actually a little bit true. I have set up my current rules of engagement and, much as they might be bonkers, they're the only ones I have. I can't abandon them at the first sight of a pair of Paul Newman eyes and some mighty fine guns, much as I'm tempted.

Something of this seriousness must come across in my tone, because Sam stops his posturing and gives me a slightly regretful smile.

'Ah,' he says. 'Well that's different, then. That actually matters.'

8

After that, Sam reduces his charm offensive to maybe a four out of ten on the official Flirtation Scale (which is a thing, by the way — Google it).

For the next few days, I see quite a lot of him, but he is noticeably less suggestive. I suspect this is a battle for him, as he is programmed to be a complete verbal tart.

Part of me is relieved. And, predictably enough, part of me is a little bit disappointed.

It does, though, give me a bit of breathing space, which I desperately needed. If Sam had kept pushing, I might well have given in. I'm only human, and I like sex. I especially like sex with tall, handsome dudes who look like they know their way around a woman.

I think he understands this, and his decision to back off is a kindness to me. Or maybe it's all part of some bigger play, who am I to know?

I don't actually know Sam very well at all, which is something we are slowly but surely addressing.

'What's your surname?' I say to him, during one of our evening strolls along the beach. 'As far as I know, your first name is Surfer, and your last name is Sam.'

'That's true,' he says, lobbing a stone into the water so perfectly that it skims and skips several steps before plunging down into the waves. 'I had it changed by deed poll.'

I make a beep-beep noise, and say: 'My lie detector just went off.'

We are both wrapped up in fleeces and both wearing big boots that are leaving firm imprints in the damp sand. The beach at this time of year is largely deserted, just a few die-hard fossil hunters and a handful of dog walkers keeping us company. I like it down here, because it's largely a Christmas-free zone — nobody has, as yet, come up with the concept of decorating the cliffs with tinsel.

'Okay. Rumbled. It's Brennan. If we got married, you'd have a great name. Becca Brennan. You'd sound like a kick-ass female private eye.'

'Well, that's assuming that I'd take your surname, isn't it? I'm quite happy with Fletcher, to be honest. I might keep it for professional reasons. And as far as you know, I'm already a kick-ass female private eye. I could be, for example, Jessica Fletcher's granddaughter.'

'Fair enough. That brings me on to my next question, then. What do you actually do, for professional reasons? Laura just said you were self-employed and spent a lot of time on your laptop.'

'I'm a tax accountant,' I lie, breezily, looking on in amusement as a Border Collie drags his unwilling owner into the edge of the sea, pulling on the lead so hard he has no choice but to follow, splashing right in up to his ankles.

'No way. Not creative enough. I'd go for . . . comedy script writer.'

'Close, but no cigar,' I reply. 'I'm actually a

best-selling author. I came up with this great series about a former major in the US military, who now roams the land as a maverick fixer, righting wrongs and balancing out injustice wherever he goes . . . '

There is a pause, where he screws up his eyes and thinks.

'Nah. I think that's Jack Reacher in the Lee Child books. I've seen pictures of Lee Child and he doesn't have boobs.'

'Oh yes. I forgot about that. I was fibbing. I'm actually a tax accountant.'

'You are so *not* a tax accountant,' he insists, passing me a flat stone so I can throw it. I skim it with zero skill and it sinks straight away. Can't win 'em all.

'Graphic designer,' I eventually admit. Not that it's shameful or anything.

'Okay. I'll settle for that one. Next question, then — you've never come close to settling down, like Laura? Punch me if that's too personal.'

I ponder the issue and decide I can allow it. As long as I don't tell the truth, it'll be fine.

'Not really. I think there were only so many domestic-goddess genes to go round in our family, and Laura got them all. I've never lasted longer than a few weeks in a relationship, not since I was a spotty teen anyway. And my overwhelming feeling when they end is always relief. You?'

'Oh, sure . . . there was Gemma Finnegan when I was sixteen. That lasted two years, until she moved away to Cork and left me with my

84

heart broken . . . then there were several years of playing around . . . then there was Suzanne, an English girl I met at college. Didn't last as long, but it was pretty intense. Then some more playing around . . . then there was Izzy, but she wanted kids when I was twenty-two and just not ready . . . and then — '

'Let me guess — there was some more playing around?'

'That's about the size of it,' he says, coming to a standstill and wiping his hands down on his jeans. He shrugs, trying to look apologetic but failing.

'I'm thirty-five now and driving my ma and sisters insane. They'd like nothing better than for me to come home, find some nice fertile local girl and start procreating.'

'Right. Sounds lovely. How do you feel about that?'

'Mixed,' he says, walking over to sit on one of the huge boulders and indicating for me to join him. 'I hate all their fussing and bossing. It's one of the main reasons I left. I'm the youngest, the only boy, and there are approximately 7,000 of them — all with kids. Seriously, I have twenty-two nieces and nephews.'

'Jesus. I wouldn't have thought they'd have had time to worry about you, then.'

'I know. But somehow, they manage to fit it in . . . don't get me wrong, I love 'em to bits. Couldn't ask for a better bunch — and we have some bloody fantastic parties. My dad died a few years back and since then I think they've wanted me home more than ever . . . and I get that, I really do. And I miss them something furious. But every time I go back, every time I'm surrounded by all the fuss and the interrogations about my love life and the endless 'isn't it time you . . . ' conversations, I feel . . . well . . . '

'Suffocated?' I suggest. 'Stifled? Strangled?'

'Yeah. Exactly that. Then I feel guilty, because I know it's because they love me. Same with you?'

'Not exactly,' I reply carefully, not meeting his eyes and gazing out to sea instead. 'They've kind of given up on me on that front.'

'Apart from Laura,' he says, nudging me. 'She still seems to be trying to find your happy ending.'

'Well, that's Laura for you. She thinks everyone should have a happy ending. She thinks everyone deserves one.'

There is a pause while he mulls this over. I am feeling a little bit exposed by this point, and tug my fleece tighter around my body, hoping I can shut the world out with a bit of help from a wool-polyester blend.

'And you don't think you deserve a happy ending?' he finally says. 'Why? What did you ever do that was so bad?'

'I push old ladies out of the way in the supermarket. And that's just when I'm in a good mood. Now come on, I'm freezing. I feel an enormous hot chocolate coming on.'

9

I spend the next weekend in Devon with Lizzie and Nate, doing Christmas shopping, eating in quaint village pubs and enjoying their company.

Lizzie was vivacious and fun, her eyes glinting with happiness between the eye-liner stripes, her step constantly buoyant and energetic. She chattered on about Josh and about school and about running the Twitter account for the Cider Cave and about Midgebo and about her GCSEs and about some girl called Alexa who has auditioned for the *X Factor* and about a million and one other things I could barely keep up with.

By the time she left Manchester in July, Lizzie had been seventy per cent sullen teen, thirty per cent little-girl-lost. Not just your normal sullen teen, but Sullen Teen With Dead Dad, which takes the potential for disaster to a whole new level. I could see the signs in her that things could easily take a very dark turn, and was genuinely worried that she'd follow similar paths to mine.

It's one of the main reasons that I, unlike my parents, never tried to talk Laura out of moving to Dorset for the summer — or, as it turned out, for ever.

I'm not blessed with psychic powers; I just knew that Lizzie needed a change. They all did — but especially her. She needed to get away from the past, find new friendships, start to believe in the future again.

Nate had always, on the surface, at least, been the easier one. He was more laid back, more pliable, less moody. Even now, as the first signs of hormones were sloshing through his ever-expanding body, he was more relaxed. The new relationships he'd found down here — especially with the menfolk of Budbury, like Matt, Frank and Sam — had been good for him.

He was getting pretty handy on the guitar thanks to Matt's lessons, he had a part-time 'job' at Frank's farm, where he hung round with Frank's grandson Luke, and he'd spent endless hours tagging along with Sam on his nature walks, surfing sessions and impromptu beach football tournaments. None of them were his dad, but they were solid, and I think David would have approved.

Nate was still a little boy in many ways — but now he had men to hang round with, who didn't fuss about his shirt not being tucked in or the fact that he'd only eaten cake for breakfast or that he had grass stains on his knees. The sudden influx of good, reliable male role models couldn't have come at a better time for him.

We stayed over on the Saturday night in a hotel near Sidmouth, where we had connecting rooms. We were tired after a busy day of shopping, walking and practising a different fake accent in each place we visited. I thought I'd scored an absolute blinder with my Aussie accent, until a girl waiting on us in a cafe on the seafront turned out to be from Sydney and I was rumbled.

We spent the night watching trashy films on the pay-per-view and eating room-service food, before I disappeared off to my own bed, where I lay awake for most of the night listening to Nate snore.

My sleeping patterns hadn't got any better since I'd come down to the South West. Not even the peace and quiet of Cherie's lovely attic flat had quite cured my insomnia, and I was barely getting enough shut-eye to function.

I was used to hiding it, though, and knew that in some ways it was a good thing. At least I was facing up to it. I'd spent many long years self-medicating in many different ways, only sleeping after a close encounter with a vodka bottle or its equivalent in male form. I'd rather be tired and coffee-dependent than go back to that.

Besides, I was glad to have been of some use to Laura. The thing with her and Matt looked to me like it was going to last the distance, but it was still relatively new. They were still discovering each other. She was still, in some ways, grieving the loss of the old, while also trying to enjoy the potential of the new.

A night alone, with no children to worry about, would do them both good — and if I had to guess, I'd say she was getting even less sleep than I was. But for far more entertaining reasons. That train of thought led me inevitably on to Sam, which led inevitably on to me opening my laptop and doing some work. Nothing quite cures horniness like trying to fit 3,000 words of copy about bin collections into a space meant for 300.

By the time we get back to Budbury, late on Sunday afternoon, I am skint, exhausted, and would quite like to lock myself in the attic for a good, solid twenty-four hours of solitude. There have been snow flurries all the way home and some of it has started to settle on the coast, like a light dusting of icing sugar on a yellow cake. We had to be careful on the drive, which frayed the last of my remaining nerves.

Willow is in the café when we get back, finishing off the cleanup from the seven customers she says she's had all day. Laura had left a small truckful of turkey sandwiches and a sinful-looking coffee and walnut cake that is only half eaten, so dinner is well and truly sorted.

I know, from Laura, that Willow cares for a mother with Alzheimer's, as well as working several jobs. You'd never, ever realise it from spending time with her. Perhaps, I think, looking at her pink hair and silver-sprayed Doc Martens and space-princess clothes, she actually has a time machine so she can zip about untroubled.

'Are you all right?' she asks, leaning against a mop and staring at me intently. I realise that I have been thinking at least some of this aloud. 'You just called me a space princess. I mean, I don't mind — that's secretly how I think of myself.'

Nate and Lizzie are sitting at one of the tables near the patio doors, also looking tired. Nate is gazing down at the bay, and Lizzie is tapping on her phone, probably texting Josh. I need to get them home to Hyacinth, but suddenly feel incapable. I'd been working on the assumption

90

that Laura would be here, for absolutely no good reason.

'Come on kids,' says Willow, propping her mop up in one corner and standing with her hands on her hips. 'Walk back with me to mine, and then I'll run you home to the cottage. Last one to the car has to do a solo of 'Let It Go' from *Frozen* . . . '

This prompts Nate and Lizzie into some frenzied action, both gathering up their backpacks and dashing for the door. Lizzie is going for the kill, but Nate pauses and gives me a dimpled smile and a wave in the doorway. Heartbreaker.

'You sure?' I ask, flooded with relief. It wasn't just the drive that was freaking me out, it was the thought of having to make small talk with Laura and Matt, in a cottage that looked like Santa's grotto.

'Positive. You look knackered. Everything here is done, just lock up after me, all right? I'll see you soon. Try and get some sleep.'

After she's gone, I drag myself up the stairs, carrying a plate of cake and try to do exactly that. Cherie's flat is a brilliantly secluded and peaceful place, a bit like an improved version of my flat back in Manchester. Both are small and set up for single living — but Cherie's has something extra. Maybe it's the views. Maybe it's the vinyl. Maybe it's the assorted knick knacks she's collected during her life.

But somehow, it has an atmosphere of calm and contentment that mine never has — probably because I live in it, and Cherie doesn't.

I dump my stuff, lay the cake plate down on the counter surface, and try very hard to ignore the fact that there is a small cupboard full of booze in the kitchen. Strange booze — odd liqueurs, vintage brandies, absinthe, foreign spirits — but booze nonetheless.

If I was a normal person, I could have a small glass of Norwegian tequila and knock myself out. But I'm not a normal person, not yet at least, so I console myself with coffee and walnut frosting instead.

After settling myself into a small nest on the sofa, wrapped in a tie-dye blanket with a glass of milk, I put on the TV. I am delighted to see before me *What's Love Got To Do With It: The Tina Turner Story*, which, with adverts, runs at almost three hours long. Perfect. The only thing that could have been better would have been *Armageddon*, a film best watched drunk, or sleep-deprived.

Eventually, I must have drifted off into snoozeland, which is often the way for me in situations like this. If I lie in bed and try to sleep, it doesn't happen — but if I give my brain permission to concentrate on something else (like the triumphant Tina finally dumping Ike, or Ben Affleck saving the world from a killer asteroid), I can fool it into relaxing.

And yes, I do realise that I talk about my own brain as though it is a separate entity to the rest of me. That's how it feels a lot of the time.

When I'm woken up some hours later, it is by the sound of my phone ringing. I have a walnut stuck to one side of my face and an empty milk glass rolling around on my lap. Tina has finished her story, and there seems to be some kind of documentary on about Thai ladyboys, with one of those women in the corner of the screen doing sign language. Bet that was a challenging gig.

I screw my eyes up in confusion and see that it is now completely dark outside. One of Cherie's windows is set slanting into the roof of the building, so it acts like a skylight. Above me is an ocean of navy blue dotted with dazzling golden stars. I feel like I am in a planetarium for a moment.

I grab my phone, which is skittering around on the table, and see a number I don't recognise. I ignore it, and concentrate on bringing myself back to consciousness, trying to remove the very squashed walnut from my skin. It doesn't want to come off, and clings like a limpet to my cheek.

The phone rings again, and I swear at it, advising it to go and do things to itself that are obviously impossible, as phones don't have arses.

I pick it up, noting that it is now 11.30pm, and hit 'answer'.

'Hey — it's me. Fancy a walk?'

It's Sam. The accent is a dead giveaway, and he sounds slightly tipsy. Monday is one of his days off, which explains that at least.

'No, I don't fancy a walk. Why are you calling me at this ungodly hour?'

I would ask how he got my number, but the answer will obviously begin with an L, end with an A, and have an AUR in the middle.

'Well I was just passing . . . '

'No you weren't. I'm in the middle of nowhere

and you live in the village, three doors down from the pub.'

'I was just passing,' he repeats, ignoring me, 'and I saw that your light was on.'

'That means nothing. I could have been asleep.'

'You're not asleep, though, are you? You're talking to me.'

'I could be sleep-talking,' I reply, straightening out my legs and shaking the cramps from my toes.

'Well, if that's the case, why don't you sleep-walk downstairs and I'll show you all the tiny nocturnal creatures that only come out at night.'

'Is that a euphemism?'

'Only if you want it to be. Though if we're going with that, forget I said tiny. Come on, Becca. Take pity on me. I'm all beered up with nowhere to go, sitting down on the beach all alone. Frank jibbed me off an hour ago, Matt's over at Laura's and I have no playmates. Take pity on a poor wee Irish lad, why don't you?'

He lays on the brogue thick as butter at that point, which does at least make me laugh.

'Five minutes,' I say, smiling. 'I need to de-walnut myself. Don't ask.'

It takes slightly longer than that, as my mind is so fuzzy I am initially bouncing off walls as I stagger around the flat trying to find my fleece. I avoid looking in a mirror, knowing that my hair will be as stylish as Donald Trump's. Besides, any man who wakes a woman up in what is — for her — the middle of the night deserves what he gets.

I take the tie-dye blanket down as well, as I know it is likely to be below freezing point outside.

I find Sam waiting on one of the boulders on the bay, stretched out flat, arms dangling loose at his sides, as though he is moon-bathing. The waves are rolling up onto the sand, frothing silver and coming close, but I assume that we are safe — him being a coastal expert and all. Although he is a drunken coastal expert, so I'll keep an eye on the situation.

I trudge towards him, glad of the blanket, and kick one of his ankles with my boot. He jerks back to life and sits up, presenting me with such a killer of a smile that I can't help but return it. He is dressed in his usual ensemble of cargo pants and fleece, and also has a woollen hat pulled down around his ears, blonde hair peeking out around the edges.

He pats his lap, as though expecting me to actually go and sit on it, and I ignore him and plonk myself down next to him on the boulder instead. The snow seems to have been washed away now, although I can still see starlight reflecting off the dusty white surfaces of the cliffs further along the coast.

'So, where are all the tiny creatures?' I say, gazing around us.

'Ah . . . well, some of them are so tiny you can't see them. Some of them you might just hear, like the occasional tawny owl. There'll be badgers around, but not on the beach. Maybe bats.'

'Mainly just drunken Irish men, then?'

'Yes. There's always at least one of those knocking around all environments, urban or rural, in my experience. Give me some of that blanket. Your hair looks interesting.'

I pass him some of the tie-dye and we end up squashed together, wrapped up in it, which was undoubtedly his plan all along.

'My hair took me hours to style, you pig. How dare you?'

He laughs and sneaks his arm around my shoulders. It is cold, and I am tired, and I give into it, leaning against him and enjoying the contact. This is harmless, I tell myself, knowing that I am possibly lying.

'This is nice,' he says, pulling me closer and sniffing my interesting hair.

'It's not disgusting,' I reply, noting his aromas too — the outdoors, woodsy shower gel, beer.

'It could be even nicer if you invited me back up to the flat, you know?' he adds, nudging me.

'Not going to happen.'

'Why not? Go on, give me one good reason. We're both consenting adults. I know you fancy me — oh yes you do, don't bother spluttering! And, you know, I'm not a complete arsehole.'

'That rules you out, then,' I say, removing the hand that has found a place on my thigh. 'I only ever sleep with complete arseholes.'

'Is that a rule, or more of a guideline?'

'A cast-iron rule. I find it's much easier that way.'

He pauses for a moment, and I wonder if he might have gone to sleep again.

'I know you're joking,' he says, eventually, in a

serious tone that makes me glad I'm not looking at him. 'But I wonder why you'd even think like that. It's all a cover, this bluster of yours, isn't it? And that includes sleeping with arseholes. Maybe if you took a chance on a nice guy, a decent guy who actually sees something in you beyond the bluster, something good would happen. Something different.'

I stay quiet. I am scared of what might come out of my mouth if I speak, and need a moment to gather my thoughts. I'm still sleepy, and I'm crushed up against a very hard male body for the first time in years, and the person who owns that body is someone who I could very easily get to like. A bit too much.

'I suppose,' I reply, when the silence has stretched to breaking point, 'that you could be right. But I'm just not ready for anything like that right now, Sam. And I know you could persuade me otherwise. I know that if you kissed me, I'd like it. I'm just asking you . . . not to. Is that okay?'

He gently strokes my hair and nuzzles into me. I can feel his breath warm on my face, and the reassuring grip of his arms around me.

'Don't worry,' he says, his voice light again — deliberately so, I know — 'I'm not going to kiss you. I've had a skinful and wouldn't be at my best.

'When I do kiss you, Becca, it'll be because we both want it, and we're both ready. And it will be an absolute cracker of a kiss, I promise.'

10

I feel like I have a bit of a hangover, which isn't really fair. I didn't get much sleep, though, after that conversation with Sam, and have now been plunged into one of my worst nightmares.

Really, it is hideous. Scary beyond belief. Stomach-churning.

I am trapped in a Christmas-themed wedding-dress shop.

The café is closed and I am here with Cherie and Laura, for no apparent reason. I would have been much happier at home, shoving my hand in a blender and pressing the 'boost' button.

Instead, I am sitting on a red-velvet chaise longue in Bath, listening to Bing Crosby tell me what colour Christmas is. The whole place is bedecked with 'tasteful' decorations — not that there is any such thing, in my opinion — and the tree is topped with a tiara and veil. It's like my own private Ida-hell.

Luckily, I think, we are nearing the end. We've had lunch — very pleasant — and the ladies have had a few drinks. I am driving, which always neatly gets me out of the drinks situation, and now they are having a final prance around in front of the mirrors.

Cherie's dress is, I have to say, perfect. Perfect for her, anyway. It's red satin, fitted in a simple Empire-line shape that flatters her larger-than-life figure. I can imagine that on Christmas Eve, when she ties the knot and has her hair and face done, she will look stunning. Like a Hollywood starlet sixty years on.

Laura, her matron of honour, is wearing a similarly plain dress in deep green, which makes her eyes pop and her figure sizzle. It's going to be one sexy wedding.

'It could be you in the wedding dress, soon, my love,' says Cherie, reaching out to tuck one of Laura's ever-stray curls behind her ear. 'You never know.'

Laura blushes, which she doesn't do that often, and looks bewildered.

'Oh, I'm not sure about that,' she mutters, defensively, which suggests to me that she has at the very least considered the possibility. I've also noticed that although she is still wearing her wedding and engagement rings, they are now on her right hand — the symbolism of which isn't lost on me. David is still part of her, but she's acknowledging the fact that she is moving on.

Personally, I can't see any reason why there won't be another wedding at some point. One look at her and Matt tells you everything you need to know — there is so much kindness there between them, so much care and respect mixed in with the naked lust. They are perfect together, and it's only their pasts holding them back.

Which, I suppose, is a sentence that could be applied to all of us, in some way or another. I have refused to join in with the fancy-dress show, or with the free champagne that is being constantly topped up by a sales assistant who seems to be already half-cut herself.

'If you and Matt do get married,' I say, sipping my coffee, 'can we do it in the Caribbean? And not at Christmas?'

'If me and Matt *do* get married,' she replies, pointing a finger at me and laughing, 'I'm going to make you wear a bridesmaid's dress that looks like a giant meringue. With hair like Cyndi Lauper in the eighties.'

'Funnily enough, that's always been a deeply held dream of mine, so bring it on . . . now, not to rush you lovely ladies or anything, but how much longer do you think we are going to be?'

'Why?' says Cherie, starting to unbutton her dress with absolutely no shame. I am told by Laura that she often walks round naked, and hope I am not about to be treated to a sneak preview of Frank's wedding night.

'Do you have a hot date you need to dash back for? I hear you were out on the beach with Surfer Sam late last night . . . '

I have absolutely zero idea how she knows this. I've not mentioned it to anybody, and as far as I know he hasn't, either. I am beginning to suspect she has some kind of giant Eye of Sauron-type affair going on at Frank's farmhouse, and uses it to keep us all under a benign state of surveillance. Cherie Moon — Big Sister.

I can tell from Laura's briefly widening eyes and the way her mouth purses into a surprised 'O', that it's news to her as well. News she likes the sound of. Bloody hell. It's like living in a romance novel with these two around.

'No, I'm just aware of the fact that it's started to snow again and somebody needs to get you

100

two old lushes home safe and sound.'

Laura peers through the velvet curtain that leads through to the main shop floor, and nods as she sees that I am right. It's falling in thick clumps, the wind blowing it around in small tornadoes and she knows that we have at least an hour and a half's drive ahead of us, even if the traffic is kind.

The girls — and despite the fact that they are both older than me, I can use no other word to describe this giddy pair — speed it up after that. The dresses are proclaimed perfect, as neither of them plans to either gain or lose huge amounts of weight in the next few weeks, and packed away along with various accessories. Willow's frock is also boxed up, on a hope-for-the-best basis as she couldn't get away long enough for the fitting.

We drive home listening to Abba's greatest hits, which is the only compromise we can reach. Laura wanted her tried-and-tested driving music, Meatloaf, and Cherie was lobbying for Bob Dylan. We all quite happily sing along to *Mamma Mia*, and arrive back in Budbury some time later.

The snow has settled a little here, but not too seriously, and I do a quick round trip to drop Cherie off at the farm and Laura at the Rockery.

I was intending to go straight back to the flat, but instead find myself just calling off at the café for supplies. For some reason, I don't want to be alone quite yet. This is an unusual feeling for me, and I have the sneaking suspicion that all of the girliness of our day has rubbed off on me.

I have made up a take-away pack of leftover smoked bacon and wild-mushroom quiche, some thick slabs of home-made granary bread and a couple of banana muffins that I know will still be fine; three portions of each. There are some distinct advantages to living above a café.

Once I'm done, I get back into the car and head for the village. It's not a long walk — probably about ten minutes along the footpaths — but I don't fancy it in the snow.

I park up by the side of the community hall, and first make a quick detour into the Pet Cemetery. I only know it's here because Lizzie told me, and I want to pay my final respects to Jimbo, Laura and David's late, great Labrador. He passed away over the summer after a long life full of sausages, chewing shoes and inappropriate farting.

The snow has settled properly in this small, square patch of remembrance, and the tiny graves and crosses are coated in white. I notice miniature paw prints and the tracks left by birds, and see a vibrant green and red holly bush giving the place some colour.

I wander aimlessly for a few minutes, collar turned up against the wind, taking a sad pleasure in reading the stories behind the graves — like Poplar, the cat who thought he was a dog; and Nibbles, the 'best rabbit that ever lived', and Dave (great name for a dog), the German Shepherd who loved snuggles.

It's a bittersweet place, melancholy and yet warm, and I say a quick prayer for Jimbo once I find him. I add in David as well, feeling slightly foolish — my religious beliefs are pretty much non-existent, but somehow I feel it is the right thing to do. I ask them both to keep an eye out for Laura and Nate and Lizzie, and even wish them a happy Christmas. Unheard of. I must be going soft in my old age.

Mission accomplished, I walk back into the main street of the village and get my bag full of food from the boot of the car. I pass the pub and the butcher's shop and the gift store and the darkened windows of the tearooms, and eventually come to the door I am looking for.

The place where, for some reason, I have been drawn on this snowy afternoon, sleep-deprived and light-headed with forced jollity. The place I think, without any evidence at all, will give me a bit of peace.

I knock on the brightly coloured door of the tiny terrace, and wait for an answer.

The door is pulled open and she stands there, all five foot nothing of her, wearing a beige cardigan and tan-coloured tights and a pair of fur-lined tartan slippers.

'Becca!' says Edie May, her face screwing up in delight. 'Come on in, my lovely — you'll catch your death out there!'

11

Edie's house, much like Edie herself, is tiny, neat and quirky. There are lots of old-lady touches — like those lacy covers on the arms of the chairs, and a toilet-roll holder in the shape of a knitted doll, and a collection of pottery shire horses. But there are also some flash gadgets that I'm sure have been provided by her extensive family of nieces and nephews and their children.

She has a cable TV box with a zillion channels — 'but never a thing to watch!' — and her own iPad, which she seems to use as a coaster. There's a telephone with huge buttons, obviously designed to help someone with ninety-year-old eyesight, and an electronic weather forecasting device that I'd quite like myself. I could press it every morning in Manchester and get told by a robotic lady voice: 'The weather is shit today.'

In one corner is a small but very exotically decorated fake Christmas tree, which screams Cherie Moon at me — because I'm not sure that Edie would have chosen to dangle glitter-sprayed ornamental gourds from the branches.

Despite never having married or had her own children — and despite the fact that she has apparently lived under the illusion that her long-dead fiance is alive and kicking for many years now; upstairs asleep at the moment, I'm told — she is clearly a much-loved and much-cherished person. I know that Cherie in particular adores her, as does Laura, and it's very easy to see why.

As she bustles around in her miniscule kitchen, she chatters away about the weather and about the wedding and about the wonderful time we're all going to have at it. She exclaims with huge joy about the food I've brought, tucking away her fiance's portion in the fridge so he can enjoy it later, and eventually settles down in an armchair so big and so squishy it looks like a throne. A very homely throne, like Edie is the Queen of Easy Living.

I am on an equally comfy sofa, a huge mug of steaming tea in front of me, along with a banana muffin. I'm not really hungry at all, and am only eating so I can keep Edie company as she pecks at her cake like a little sparrow.

'So,' she says, after she's licked her wrinkled fingertips free of crumbs, 'how are you enjoying your time here, my lovely? Getting plenty of rest?'

The way her eyes flicker over me tells me she suspects otherwise. That, given the dark circles under my eyes and my zombie-like state, would probably not take a genius to figure out. Still, she looks a bit like Miss Marple, so I automatically respect her detective skills.

'I'm not very much into rest,' I reply, leaning back into the hug of the sofa and giving her what I hope is a reassuring smile.

'No, I see that. A restless soul! But, you see, things are different here. You're away from your real life now. All you have to do is give it a chance, and I'm sure something magical will happen.'

Hmmm. I fight back a comment about magically reappearing fiancés, because that would be cruel and unnecessary. Edie, to be fair, has lived for nine whole decades of Budbury life and probably knows more than I do. About everything, ever.

'I'm not sure about magic, really, Edie. To be honest, I'd settle for a good night's sleep.'

'Oh yes. One of the most under-estimated joys of life, a good night's sleep. Is there anything in particular keeping you awake? Anything you want to talk about? I'm just an old lady, but I'm good at listening . . . and I can keep a secret, my sweet, don't you worry about that. Carry them on my back like a snail, I do, all the secrets I've been told over the years.'

I have no doubt about that at all. And the shrewd look in her eyes tells me that she might be 'just an old lady', but she's also so much more than that. She's . . . a safe haven. A safe haven in fluffy slippers. I have no idea why I feel like that about Edie — whether it's just her age, or her life experience, or her super-soft sofa, or the fact that she's kept on going even though she's just a little bit broken. But since the day we met, I've felt like I could trust her.

Like I have a connection with her, in the same way that Laura clearly feels about Cherie. It's odd that Laura — safe, solid Laura — should end up with a rock-chick hippy pensioner as her mentor, and I get the supergran, but there you go.

I sip my tea, and look at Edie, and listen to the companionable silence of her little home. I can feel words rising to the surface, and wonder if subconsciously, that's why I made this trip in the first place — why I drove to see Edie instead of going back to bed. If some small, inarticulate part of my mind told me that today was the day I needed to talk. To acknowledge.

I feel the words rising, and they are words I've never, ever spoken out loud before. Words that belong to stories I've never told. Words that describe the hurt I've never expressed. Words that probably won't capture the guilt I've never properly climbed over. I feel them there, these words, powerful, bubbling under the surface like lava, scalding hot and searingly painful.

Edie stays quiet, letting me think it through. Letting me breathe. Letting me decide whether to talk, or to do what I've always done, and gloss over the past.

'I don't know, Edie,' I say, eventually. 'I'm about as good at talking as I am at resting. I've never been one for discussing my feelings. I prefer to pretend I don't have them.'

She nods, and places her china cup down on its saucer. She got a china cup painted with hedgehogs, I got a giant builders' mug. She obviously thought I needed it.

'And how's that working out for you?' she replies, one furry white eyebrow cocked upwards in a question. I can't help but smile. She's a sly old fox, Edie.

'It's working out ... not so brilliantly, I suppose. Which has kind of been fine up until now. But for some reason, now, I feel . . . bad. Like something different needs to happen. And I'm not used to different. I'm not sure I could cope.'

'You're at a crossroads, you see,' says Edie. 'That's the magical thing that's going to happen while you're here.'

'It doesn't feel very magical, though. It feels . . . awful.'

I realise as I say it that it's true. I do feel awful. Not just in the common-or-garden way I usually feel awful — sleep-deprived, borderline exhausted, cynical, stressed, lonely. I'm used to all of that. That's my default setting. This, this feeling I have right now as I sit in this tiny terraced house being scrutinised by someone I barely know, is a whole new level of awful.

Perhaps it's being so involved in other people's lives that's done it. Being here, seeing Laura in her new glory, seeing the way she is connected to Matt and Cherie and Frank and the café.

Seeing Lizzie and Nate moving on and grow-ing up. Seeing the way this whole community loves and supports each other. Meeting Sam, the big lummox. Seeing all of this wonderful living going on around me — so bright and comforting and joyous — and still feeling like I simply can't join in with it. That I can fake my way through it for a few weeks, but that it will never be mine.

That I simply don't deserve it. That I'm a charlatan, a fraud, a loser — and that these people would be better off without me.

I feel big, fat, self-pitying tears sliding out of my eyes, and am momentarily confused by what is happening. I am not one of life's criers — unlike Laura, who is a blubbering princess — I've always been inclined to keep my emotions inside. Because, you know, if I let them out, they might be like baboons escaping from the zoo — they'll go on a noisy rampage and snap car aerials off and show everybody their bright red bums.

Edie reaches out, and gives my hand a little pat. Her skin is papery and soft, and her touch is reassuring. It pulls me back into the real world, and away from the scary landscape of my internal life. Baboons, for goodness' sake!

'It's good to have a little cry now and then,' she says, simply. 'Does you the world of good.'

I just nod, and have little choice but to agree with her and hope she's right — because the tears show no sign of stopping, whether I want them to or not. At least they're just quietly getting on with it, not making me sob or snort snot or anything. Small mercies.

'Something bad happened to me, a long time ago,' I say, aware of how silly that must sound to Edie, to whom very bad things had happened a very long time ago. 'And I just don't seem able to quite get past it.'

'Well, that's a thing I can understand, child. Some things just feel too big and too bad to get past, don't they? Like if you even try, you're betraying a memory.'

I nod, reminded once again that I brought an extra portion of quiche and cake for her long-gone lover. No, Edie hadn't got past her own personal tragedy — but she seemed to have found a way to work around it. To live with it.

Maybe that's the best I could hope for. Maybe that's why fate put her in my path — she'll be my Mrs Miyagi of Screwed-Up-But-Viable-Living.

'What happened, if you don't mind me asking?' she says quietly, leaning back in her chair so she's not crowding me. 'And tell me to mind my own beeswax if you like.'

'No, no, it's fine . . . maybe I need to talk about it. And what's the worst that can happen, right?'

Edie raises her eyebrows at that, and I have to laugh. And cry. Both at the same time, which is pretty confusing.

'It was when I was seventeen,' I explain, gazing off towards the window that overlooks the main street through the village. I might be able to make myself talk about it, but I won't be able to look at her at the same time. The only way I can do this is by somehow pretending I'm just talking out loud to an empty room. So I stare out, at the fresh-falling snow and the passers-by huddling into their winter coats, and I talk.

'I was just seventeen and I was in love. In that way you can only be when you're that age — completely and utterly and totally. I'd always been a bit of a . . . well, the diplomatic word would probably be a 'handful'. I never did what I was supposed to, even if it was what I wanted to do all along . . . it just seemed to be part of me to be awkward. I never felt like I fitted in, even with my own family, and then when I met Shaun . . . well, suddenly I did fit in. It was the whole 'you complete me' thing that you're always looking for at that age . . . maybe any age, I don't know . . .

'Anyway. Long story short, after a couple of months together, I got pregnant. I know now, looking back, that I was an idiot. That I shouldn't have been sleeping with him — or with anyone, I was just a kid. But of course I *loved* him, and I thought I was grown up, and Laura had David and they were so happy, and maybe I thought it would all work out like that for me as well.

'So, well, yeah. I was an idiot. When I found out I was pregnant, I thought — I genuinely, stupidly thought — that he'd be happy about it. That we'd go off and get a little flat together, and I'd escape my family, and we'd raise this little person in complete harmony. That we'd go to festivals with our cute toddler and I'd make hummus and he'd have a job as a park ranger or something, and that we'd live this fabulous Bohemian life. Shaun was pretty alternative — he had a nose ring before they were even cool — so I assumed he'd be alternative in the way he wanted to live, not just the way he dressed. That my weird and wacky vision of our future would be just as appealing to him as it was to me.'

I pause there, simply because I have to. The memories are still so real, and still cut so deep, that it feels like it's happening to me all over again. Phantom pain.

We'd met in the park near our house. He brought the cider and the fags, expecting a party. I brought the pee-stick, expecting a celebration. Expecting him to take me in his manly arms, and come out with a line that a boy from a film would come out with: 'Don't worry, Becca, I love you — together, we can take on the world/or something like that.

Instead, he just went pale. Chugged down half a bottle of Strongbow. Lit up a cigarette with shaking hands.

And said: 'You'll have to get rid of it. My dad'll kill me if he finds out.'

Even now, all these years later, I still feel the sting of those words. Even now, completely understanding and forgiving him for that perfectly natural teenaged boy reaction to terrifyingly big news, I still feel the swirl of nausea in the pit of my stomach.

The slap of the rejection, the confusion, the horror as reality started to slowly dawn on me. The shockwaves that slammed through me as I started to grasp that there was a huge gap between my expectations of what would happen and what was actually happening.

I can still feel the fear and loneliness as I watched him walk away, baggy jeans hanging low on his skinny hips, disappearing off between the swings and the roundabout in a cloud of Marlboro Lights.

He was a kid. I really, really don't hold it against him. Not now. But back then? Back then I felt like my whole world had been destroyed. Like I would never breathe again. Like I wanted to die.

'But I take it you didn't get a little flat together?' asks Edie, reminding me that I am not alone. At least not physically.

'No. In fact I never spoke to him again. He avoided me at school, dumped me by text and got a new girlfriend within days. It was brutal. I suppose I probably would have recovered from all of that — most girls do — but I wasn't only dumped, I was dumped and pregnant. I was feeling terrible in every possible way — physically, emotionally. Just a total wreck. I couldn't talk to Laura about it — although I know now, with hindsight, that I should have. I couldn't back then. Or my parents. I was so . . . embarrassed. Humiliated. And so bloody desperate.

'I had no idea what to do. I had nobody I felt I could turn to. And I . . . well, I genuinely considered killing myself, Edie. It makes me shiver now, but I did. I'd sit and look at pictures of people like Kurt Cobain on my bedroom wall — '

She looks confused, and I don't blame her.

'Dead pop star. Don't worry, it's not relevant. Anyway, In the end, after a few weeks of pure, undiluted misery, where I'm sure I put my entire family through hell, I decided to go and see someone at a family planning clinic in the city. I still remember the bus ride into town — huddled on the back seat, glaring at anyone who looked like they were going to sit by me, freezing cold and terrified. Everybody else thinking about Christmas shopping and me thinking about death.

'The people at the clinic were lovely — they were kind to me, even when I was not an easy person to be kind to. The nurse explained my 'options' — keeping the baby, considering adoption or booking me in for a termination.

Everything was done so professionally, and they were so understanding — but it was still terrible. None of those options were appealing. The only option I could see was either me not existing any more or inventing a time machine and going back to undo it all.

'I tried to contact Shaun, to see what he thought. I told myself it was because he had a right to know, but, to be truthful, I think I was still pathetically hoping that he'd come to my rescue somehow. That we'd get back together and, against the odds, I'd be happy again. He never even replied — I was well and truly on my own.'

'Oh, you poor girl,' Edie whispers, and I see her crinkled eyes have also filled with tears. Part of me had wondered if Edie — a lady of the older generation — would be judgemental of my frankly immoral behaviour, but I was grateful to see that she wasn't. 'What did you do?'

'I lay in bed, night after night, praying to a God I wasn't sure I even believed in. And I didn't pray for anything worthy, like world peace or an end to famine, I prayed that he would take my baby away, or take me away. That he'd make it *all* go away. That he'd make an aeroplane fall on my head on the way to school, just to put me out of my misery. I'll . . . I'll never forgive myself, Edie. Because the week after, it happened. Not the aeroplane thing, but . . . the baby. I lost the baby.

'I was at school when it happened. I won't go into details, it's too horrible. But it happened and I went home saying I had a tummy bug, and I locked myself in my room and I cried and I cried and I cried. I was in a lot of pain, physically, which I was trying to ignore — I felt like I deserved it, do you know what I mean? Like it was my punishment for being such a terrible person. For being the type of girl who wished for such terrible things.

'Eventually, I had to go back to the clinic, and go through some awful procedure at hospital, just before Christmas — worst Christmas ever — and I did it all alone. Because that, too, was part of my punishment. I think, in some ways, that's what I've been doing ever since, in different ways. Punishing myself.'

Edie is silent for a while, and I concentrate on what is going on outside. I see people walking past, umbrellas flying in the wind, carrying plastic bags and probably wondering what they're going to cook for tea and thinking about their Christmas shopping. I see cars slowly driving through the village, and the snow still falling. Out there, life goes on.

In here, it feels like it's stopped.

'I'm so sorry that happened to you, my love,' says Edie, eventually. 'It's a terrible thing to have gone through, all alone, when you were so very young. But you can't keep blaming yourself, not after all this time. I'm not sure, after all these years, if I believe in God either — but I'm very sure that if He does exist, He doesn't take babies away from confused children who don't know how to cope. And that's what you were, isn't it? Just a child?'

'I know. And I've told myself that over and over again, but . . . well, nothing changes. It's still there, always. It's like part of me just stopped right then, when I was seventeen and suffering. Just frozen still. And I have no clue how to deal with that. I think part of me has been grieving that loss ever since it happened, no matter how much I'd wished for it.

'I've tried to build a life for myself, but I always find myself wondering what it would have been like if things had been different . . . if it would have been a boy or a girl. If it would be lovely like Laura, or a pain in the arse like me . . . whether it was a blessing in disguise, or a curse . . . '

'Well,' Edie continues, wiping a tear from beneath her eye. 'That's only natural. None of us live our lives without the might-have-beens, do we? But imagine if, heaven forbid, such a thing were ever to happen to your Lizzie. What would you say to her?'

I feel a clutch of fear in my stomach at the thought of Lizzie going through what I went through, and make a mental note to at least try and have a few awkward conversations with her. I've seen the way she looks at Josh and the way he looks at her, and . . . well, it's both lovely and terrifying at the same time.

'I think,' I reply, 'that I'd tell her to talk about it. To not suffer alone. To forgive herself. And I'd give her the world's biggest cuddle.'

Edie stands slowly to her feet, and picks up my mug of now cold tea.

'I'd think that would be exactly the right way to react,' she says over her shoulder as she walks to kitchen.

'And I think that's exactly what you should do for yourself, as well.'

12

I feel exhausted after all of that, and Edie immediately picks up on it. Wise old owl. She forces me to eat a slice of quiche, and replenishes my mug of tea, and gives me a tartan blanket to throw over my legs. I'm not cold, but I take it for what it is — a sign of comfort.

'I think,' I say, as I snuggle under the fleece, 'that I am all talked-out now, Edie. Thanks very much for listening. I know it's not a pleasant story. I half expected you to show me the door.'

'Don't be so silly, Becca. There's nothing to thank me for. We're all fragile creatures in our own way, and you're not the first person to sit on that sofa and cry, not by a long shot. One of few advantages of reaching my age is that I've seen it all. Learned not to judge anyone until I've walked in their shoes. That's why we all need friends, isn't it, to help us out with the weak spots? And sometimes the weak spots nobody can see are the ones that hurt the most.'

That almost has me crying again. She is so kind, so generous, so understanding. I know that Laura's move to Dorset started as something desperate, something hopeful but unsure, with her whole future dominated by her past — but somehow, she's moved on.

She's found herself again. She's bright and bubbly and optimistic — and she'd done that with the help of Cherie and Edie and Matt and

Frank and the whole family that the Comfort Food Café has provided her with.

She's been enveloped in their love and humour and concern, and now she's back on track, as are Nate and Lizzie. I feel a tiny flickering of hope that maybe, just maybe, it can do the same for me. That Edie is right, and something magical might just happen.

I am pathetically grateful for the comfort of this small house, and this small old lady, and the huge gift she's given me — the gift of hope.

Just then, she decides to almost ruin it all.

'Now,' she says, grinning at me with glee, 'I think we need to lighten our spirits a bit, don't you? Do you like *Strictly Come Dancing*? Of course you do, everyone does! I have all of them here, and I think we should settle in and watch a bit of it . . . nothing like a nice cha-cha-cha and a bit of glamour to cheer you up!'

She trots over to her collection and starts to flick through the discs.

'Which series?' I mumble, between sips of tea. I am not a huge fan — but it's the least I can do. She's listened to my tales of woe, and if that means I have to laugh at Len Goodman joking about pickling his walnuts, it's still a good deal.

'I think,' she replies, holding a box up triumphantly, 'an old one — the one where Mark Ramprakash does that lovely rhumba and goes on to win it.'

'Edie, you've spoiled the ending now!'

She giggles like a schoolgirl, pops in the disc, and the show begins. Unlikely as it might seem, it turns out to be one of the most peaceful evenings I've had in my entire life. Edie provides an insightful commentary as we watch, talking about her glory days at tea dances and the way her dad taught her to waltz when she was little and making 'ooooh' noises at the more revealing outfits.

She comes out with classic comments, like 'Mutton. Lamb. That's all I'm saying', and 'That Craig Revel Horwood must have been dropped on his head as a child', and 'I think Arlene's been drinking her bitchy juice this evening' — even though she's obviously seen this a thousand times.

She sighs over 'lovely' Anton du Beke every time he appears, and calls Len a 'silver fox', and generally makes the whole thing much more entertaining than I could ever have imagined it could be. Honestly, she's so funny, they should have her on *Gogglebox*.

Perhaps I am feeling extra relaxed after my big confessional. Perhaps watching Peter Schmeichel try and turn his rigid body into a dancer's grace is especially cathartic. I don't know what it is — but eventually, I drift off to sleep.

I don't realise this at the time, of course — I am too busy nodding off to acknowledge it happening. But as I come back to consciousness, spread out over the whole of the sofa, covered in the tartan blanket, face coated elegantly in snoring drool, I feel . . . wonderful. Rested. Relieved. Ready to face the day.

It is the first solid stretch of sleep that I have had since David died and I decided to quit all my vices cold turkey. Perhaps this was the answer after all my struggles — get rid of the vodka and the men, and simply replace them with old episodes of *Strictly Come Dancing*. The way I feel, it should be made available on prescription.

My eyes feel alert — as opposed to their usual dry, exhausted, stuck-together state — and my first thought isn't 'ugggh, I want to die, where's the coffee?'

My first thought, as I look around me at the darkened living room, light creeping through the now-drawn curtains, is 'thank God for that.'

I know having a good night's sleep doesn't sound that exciting. It's not on most party girls' list of Top Ten Things To Do. But for me, it feels amazing — like I can think again. Breathe again. Manage to not only get through a day, but try and even enjoy it. I feel like I could run up Everest and train-surf the roof of the Orient Express and beat Serena Williams on centre court at Wimbledon, all with energy to spare.

I stretch my arms out over my head, which is a much bigger display of physical prowess than I can usually manage in the morning, and sit upright. I glance around, and see that Edie is still here with me. She is asleep in her big armchair throne, a matching tartan blanket over her frail legs, looking like she belongs in a home for elderly angels.

She isn't snoring, or drooling. She looks really peaceful, and totally still. This freaks me out as I suddenly remember that Edie is ninety years old and has definitely reached the stage in her life where waking up in the morning is something you should never take for granted. In fact, she is so still, so silent, so pale, that I could almost believe she was dead . . .

I jump up, almost tripping over the blanket as it falls to the floor, and dash over to her. I'm not sure what I should be doing — checking for a pulse, holding a small mirror in front of her face, whipping out a non-existent stethoscope?

I settle for shaking her slightly by her narrow shoulders and shouting: 'Edie! Edie, are you all right?'

Okay, it probably wouldn't win me any Healthcare Professional of the Year awards, but I am swamped with relief when she shudders back to life and looks up at me, squinting in understandable confusion.

'Yes, dear?' she says, giving my hand a little pat. 'Is it time for another cuppa?'

13

I return to the Comfort Food Café to find Willow in the middle of a rush. At this time of year, a rush is anything more than three tables full of customers. The main tourist season runs from Easter to the end of summer, but plenty of people still come down for autumn and for Christmas — they just don't necessarily want to visit a windswept cafe perched on the side of a cliff.

The snow didn't settle overnight, and the footpaths have taken on a muddy tinge, the beach a deep shade of beige as the tide sweeps in. It's cold, and damp, and fairly miserable — but the weather does nothing to detract from the fact that I feel great.

I walk into the cafe and see Cherie and Frank at one table. I can tell from the fact that Cherie is wearing her apron that she's been helping out with the cooking and is now enjoying a cuppa with her sprightly fiancé. He might be eighty, but he's fit as the proverbial Stradivarius and still a good-looking man. They make a handsome couple, like a cover shot for *Saga* or something.

I know, from Laura's stories over the summer, that Frank lost his wife a few years ago. She'd always made him burnt bacon butties and builders' tea for his breakfast, and after he lost her, he started coming to the café — where his comfort food of choice, that exact same brekkie, was prepared for him by Cherie and later by my sister.

Cherie, who was also a widow, had looked after him when he needed her. In the same way she looked after Laura, and Lizzie and Nate, and the way she looks after Willow and Edie and so many more people here. She's a one-woman care machine.

I wander over to their table, and give her a kiss on the cheek. Just because I feel like it.

'Now, now,' says Frank, winking at me with one sparkling blue eye, 'that's my wife-to-be you're interfering with, there. Don't be coming round here with your saucy city ways.'

'I'm pretty sure Cherie could teach me a thing or two about sauce, Frank,' I reply, glancing around at the rest of the 'crowd'.

There is another elderly couple two tables over, both reading different sections of the newspaper and nibbling on toast; Ivy Wellkettle, who runs the local pharmacy, with her daughter Sophie; a pair of teenagers who have huge backpacks and look like they might be Spanish or Italian, and a lone mum sitting with a resigned look on her face as her toddler throws his toast soldiers on the floor. She isn't eating herself, just repeatedly picking up the bread, and trying not to look like she's struggling. Poor thing, she looks knackered.

'That I could,' says Cherie, 'but I don't want to be sharing all my secrets now, do I? Not with Frank here. A woman's got to keep some sense of mystery about her.'

'You'll always be a mystery to me, my love,'

answers Frank, standing up and preparing to leave. 'Now, I'd best be off. I've left Luke on his own in charge of the farm and I fear for his safety. Some of those cows had wild eyes this morning. I'll see you ladies later.'

He leans down to kiss Cherie — it's obviously her lucky day — and strides away.

I am still looking at the young mum, as is Cherie, now. She has long, straggly blonde hair that hasn't seen a salon in years, and looks utterly defeated by life. The baby is male, from his clothes, and is full of all the energy his mum seems to have lost. I've seen this before, this transferral of vitality from mother to child, like the kid is a super-cute parasite in a bobble hat.

'Looks done in, doesn't she, poor lamb?' says Cherie, sipping her coffee and gazing at me over the steam. 'Willow's finishing off the breakfast orders for the young ones over there, and I'm resting my old legs. Be a poppet and see if she needs any help?'

It's the sort of challenge I'd normally shy away from. Apart from Lizzie and Nate, I've never had much to do with kids. I'm fine with them once they can talk and appreciate sarcasm, but younger than that and they slightly freak me out. I don't know how much of this is connected to the baby I lost, and how much of it is simply that I'm not a very maternal person.

But this morning, pumped up and full of viv, I feel up to it. I nod, and walk over to the woman and her son.

'Hi,' I say, leaning down to pick up another discarded piece of toast from the floor and adding it to the pile on the table. 'Can I get you something to eat? It looks like this little fella has had enough . . . '

The toddler looks up at me from his high-chair prison and gives me a challenging glare that immediately results in me nicknaming him Damien. Silently, of course.

'Oh! No! I . . . I'm sorry for the mess,' his mum replies, looking horrified at me being near her. I try not to take it personally. She has the rabbit-in-headlights expression of the sleep-deprived and fragile.

'Don't be daft. Better he makes a mess here than at home, eh? How old is he?'

Her face immediately lights up as she starts to talk about the baby, telling me that he's eighteen months old, called Saul, and that he's 'quite the character'. This, I understand, is a euphemism for 'a complete bloody nightmare' — but the mother code doesn't allow her to say that out loud.

'Well,' I reply, once she's filled me in, 'you'd be doing us a favour if you at least had some toast for yourself as well. We've got too much bread in today, and it'll only get thrown away if we don't use it. Go on, let me get you some — on the house.'

She still looks wary and nervous, but eventually nods her head and gives me a little smile. Saul is now happily mashing up his boiled egg with a spoon, tiny bits of shell ricocheting around him like shrapnel after a land mine's exploded.

I smile at them both, narrowly dodge a glob of

egg yolk, and make my way through to the kitchen, where I greet Willow.

Willow is dressed in black today, modelling a very dustbin-chic outfit that uses a lot of netting and torn lace. Her pink hair is wild and free, and she has three sets of studs in one ear and none in the other. She's plating up food for the tourist types, and looking confused by it.

'They wanted tuna paninis,' she says, frowning. 'At this time in the morning! And they took about sixteen of the little pots of cream for their coffee.'

'Hmmm,' I say, casting a glance back out into the cafe. 'Maybe they're were-cats?'

Her whole face changes, as though I have just solved all the mysteries of the universe at once.

'That must be it! You okay to help out for a bit if we get anyone else in? Laura's off sorting something for Cherie's hen night, and we've been busier than usual. I have to get straight back to my mum as soon as lunch is done.'

'Of course,' I reply, putting a couple of slices of home-baked granary bread into the industrial-sized toaster. 'Not a problem.' I really am Miss Congeniality today.

By the time Willow has delivered supplies to the Euro were-cats and the toast is done, Cherie has also decided to introduce herself to the young mum. I see that she has the demonic toddler in her arms and is walking him around the café showing him the various strange items hanging from the ceiling and letting him grab hold of mobiles with his pudgy hands.

I put the toast on the young mum's table, with

some jam and butter and a coffee refill, and let her be. She looks like she needs a bit of time on her own, and even though she is watching Cherie and Saul as they make their slow turns around the room, I can see her visibly relax. Her breathing comes slower and deeper, and she stops biting her fingernails.

I make myself busy in the kitchen, carrying out tasks that Willow sets me, preparing salads and slicing up cheesecakes and checking the supplies for the monstrously large and decadent hot chocolates that seem to sell so well in this weather. I only eat a couple of the Flakes, which I think is quite restrained of me.

The mum and her baby, after about twenty minutes of peace that seems to have recharged her batteries, eventually leave. She straps him up in his pushchair, so bundled in a padded jacket and his hat that only a few inches of his face are peeking through, and waves as she goes.

Cherie brings the plates over, and passes them to me to stack in the dishwasher.

'Poor thing,' she says, grabbing a cloth to wipe down the table with. 'Exhausted, she is. She's called Katie, and she's just moved here from Bristol. Doesn't seem to be a dad on the scene, and I suspect, from the state of her nerves, that there's something not very pleasant gone on there. Didn't get the whole story — but she'll be back. We'll make sure they're all right. Found out she has a bit of a thing for school-dinner puddings, roly poly and the like . . . maybe they remind her of simpler times. We'll get on the case and make sure there's some spotted dick waiting for her next time she calls in.'

As she says this, Cherie gives me a brilliantly saucy wink, which makes me laugh out loud. This, I think, watching as Katie and Saul make their way carefully down the hill, is what the Comfort Food Café is all about — helping people. And feeding them cake. Which, now I come to ponder it, pretty much amounts to the same thing anyway.

'And how are you getting on, love?' Cherie asks, leaning on the counter and raising her eyebrows at me.

'I,' I reply, pausing in my kitchen duties to give her a grin, 'haven't felt this good in years, to be honest, Cherie. I went round to see Edie and we ended up having a party. Stayed up all night.'

'*Strictly Come Dancing* marathon?' she asks, knowingly. I see I am not the first person to be trapped in Edie's evil glitterball web.

'Yes. That and a lot of tea. She's . . . amazing, isn't she?'

'That she is, darling. Can't imagine this place without her. Ready for the hen night this weekend?'

I wrinkle my nose up as I consider that question. The hen night and the stag do are taking place at the same hotel, a country house type of affair out in the wilds of nowhere. This is, of course, an unorthodox set-up — but unorthodox is very much Cherie's way.

Scrumpy Joe Jones, who runs the cider cave where Lizzie works, will be coming, but his wife Joanne — who is anti-social and proud of it — isn't, so Lizzie and Nate are staying there for the night, along with Midge. As Joanne is possibly the most frighteningly stern woman I've ever met, I have no doubt at all that Josh and Lizzie will be doing no illicit sneaking around rooms in the night.

We — the Hens — will be having spa treatments and champagne teas, and the menfolk will be shooting clay pigeons and doing archery and drinking themselves stupid.

I might be feeling good today, but I am still slightly overwhelmed by the thought of being trapped in a building with so many people — even if one of them is my sister.

'Truth?' I ask, giving the surface a vigorous wipe over, Cherie holding her arms up so I can reach it all.

'Always,' she replies.

'Bit freaked out. I mean, you're all lovely and everything, but . . . '

'But there are a lot of us? And we'll all be drunk and leery and dancing to Christmas songs in a big circle in a tinsel-coated function room?'

'Well, I hadn't even considered that possible scenario, but yes — I'm not a very Christmassy person.'

'I'd noticed that,' Cherie replies, looking out at her customers rather than directly at me. Giving me a little space, I think, 'Any particular reason?'

'Long story. Long story, combined with natural grumpiness.'

'Well, maybe you'll tell me one day, eh?' she asks, giving me a confident smile that leaves me in no doubt at all that she thinks I will. And she's probably right. But there are other people to tell first — like my sister.

'Anyway,' she says, standing up straight and running her hands over her apron. 'I best go and check on Ivy and the others while Willow has a break. Plus you'd better get a Pot Noodle out — Surfer Sam's about to ask you for one . . . '

'How do you know? Are you using your sixth sense?'

'No,' she replies, smirking as she walks away, 'one of my original five. I just saw him jogging up the hill.'

Sure enough, seconds later Sam bursts through the doors in a cloud of steam. He's wearing a gilet over that lycra running gear that keeps you warm in all weathers, and which also, I can't help but notice, clings to absolutely every visible muscle in his body. Which is quite a lot of muscle.

He looks super-fit and super-tall and so all-round super that I suck in a bit of air as he approaches me, a broad smile on his face, blue eyes sparkling. His blonde hair is damp, from the drizzle and from his exertions, and he looks tired but happy. I'm told exercise can do that for you, but so far in life I've never been tempted to find out.

'Yo! Becca!' he says, his attempt at an American accent completely swamped by his natural Irish. 'Get the kettle on, woman — I'm needing me a big old pot of noodles!'

I laugh and roll my eyes, and get a chicken-and-mushroom flavour from the cup-board, where Cherie keeps a stash of them just for Sam. Pot Noodles are his comfort food, I know from Laura — a reminder of home, where he and his multitude of sisters used to have them as a Saturday treat to give his mum a break from the endless cooking.

I smash it up a bit with a fork, and add the boiling water. It smells alarmingly good, and I decide that I'll have one for my tea tonight as well.

Cherie bustles over towards us, and sniffs Sam experimentally.

'No hugs for you today, my sweet,' she says, heading back behind the counter.

'Ah, come on — give a man a break!' he says, giving her big, fake sad eyes. 'I'm just staying in shape for you, Cherie — it's not too late to dump Frank, you know, and go cougar!'

Cherie guffaws at this, and shoos me out of the kitchen.

'Go. We can cope just fine for a bit. Take this man away from me before I give in to temptation.'

Sam flexes his arms to make his biceps pop, which I know is a comedic move, but still makes me close my eyes and count to ten. Maybe it's my good night's sleep. Maybe it's pouring my heart out to Edie. But I am feeling incredibly . . . frisky, this morning.

He gestures to a table in the corner, and I follow him over, clutching a fresh coffee and nodding to Ivy and Sophie as we pass. I notice Sophie, who is twenty and home from university for Christmas, eyeing him up as we go by, and can't really blame her. He's quite the specimen as he takes off his body-warmer and unfurls himself into a chair.

I sit down, and stay quiet, fearing that if I speak, I might suggest something inappropriate involving a can of squirty cream.

'You're looking at me funny,' he says, as he stirs his Pot Noodle and takes his first mouthful. A look of pure bliss crosses his face. He's easily pleased.

'Am I?' I ask, leaning back and crossing my arms over my chest.

'Yep. You're looking at me . . . lustfully. I suspect you're having dirty thoughts.'

'I cannot confirm or deny that accusation,' I reply.

'You're looking at me lustfully because I am a well-fit Irish stud muffin.'

'That might be true. But you're currently a well-fit Irish stud muffin with Pot Noodle hanging out of the corner of his mouth.'

He wipes his face and laughs, not in the slightest bit embarrassed. I like that about him. I like most things about him, I realise — not just the way he looks, but the way he smiles and jokes with everyone. His honesty and openness and his love of all things to do with his job. The way he simply seems to make people feel better, just by being around. I've known him for less than a fortnight and already know I will miss him when I get home.

'Been for a run,' he says, after a few more moments of eating.

'I guessed that,' I answer. 'I'm quite the detective.'

'Bit sweaty now. Going home for a shower. You

132

could always come with me, if you want to wash some of those dirty thoughts away . . . it's big enough for two.'

I smile at him and shake my head. The thought of Sam naked, running water splashing over those broad shoulders, over the pretty hot tattoos I know he has under that lycra top, is not a displeasing one. But . . . well. No.

'I appreciate the offer,' I say, biting my lip a little as I look at him. I'm feeling a bit nervous, but decide to push on. Opening up to Edie has done me the world of good, so I might as well see if I'm on a roll.

'The thing is, Sam . . . '

I pause, trying to choose the right words, and he pauses along with me, putting his fork down and pushing the pot away.

'Yes?' he says, after the pause seems to transform into a complete full stop. 'What is the thing, Becca? Go on. Joking aside, you can trust me. What is the thing?'

I am at a crossroads here. I know I could say something random, like 'the thing is, I have a hot date with Sylvester Stallone this morning', or 'the thing is, I'm like the Wicked Witch of the West, and I dissolve under running water'. I know he'd understand, that he'd appreciate I was stalling, and that he'd let me. He's a very gentle soul beneath the charm.

But also . . . I could not do that. I could do as he says and trust him. That's not something I normally do — but as Edie pointed out the night before, my 'normal' just doesn't seem to be working out too well for me any more. I sigh out my indecision and take a leap of faith.

'I've had problems, over the years, you know,' I say, holding the coffee mug like a comforter as I meet his eyes. They're blue and kind and looking at me very intensely. 'With all sorts of things. Too many recreational drugs. Too much booze. Too many meaningless relationships . . . '

He simply nods, and lets me catch my breath before I continue.

'But I kind of gave it all up, a few years ago. All of it. At once. And in my mind, it's all connected — a whole pattern of behaviour that I'm trying to leave behind. A package deal I want rid of. So, I might be bonkers — in fact I am — but if I have a drink, I feel like I won't stop. If I have a puff of one of those special cigarettes we all know Cherie has, I'll be lost. And if I get in the shower with you, Sam . . . '

'Then you think it'll all come tumbling back down on you.'

'Exactly. At the moment, all my vices are still too tied in with each other. I hope, one day, that I'll be able to separate them all out. Have a glass of wine. Have a . . . well, spend the night with someone. But at the moment, I'm just not sure enough of myself to risk it. Does any of that make any sense at all?'

He's silent for a moment, looking through the windows down to the sea. Then he reaches out, and places his hand over mine. It stays there, gentle and tender, until he gives it a quick squeeze and smiles at me.

'Bizarrely, it does make sense. I think you're under-estimating yourself, and I think that at some point, you're going to have to test some of those theories out. Self-control like that can only last so long. But I understand. And much as I'd like to whisk you back home with me, I get what you're saying, and why you're saying it. You're safe with me, Becca. Because while I might come across as a bit of a lightweight, I'd never mess with anyone's mental health. It's too precious. I'm glad you told me, and I'd like you to know just one thing.'

'What's that?'

'That I'm here if you need me. And no, before you say it, I don't mean if you decide you need a one-night stand — although hey, I'm only flesh and blood, and I probably wouldn't say no — I mean if you need to talk about it. Or if something goes wrong, and you fall off that tower you've got yourself perched on, all alone. Just promise me that if it does, if you need help, you'll come and get me, okay? Because you're not in Manchester now. You're here, with us, and you don't actually need to do it all alone, all right?'

I'm feeling a little teary-eyed by this point, and am also conscious of the fact that Cherie and Willow are pretending to chat among themselves by the counter, but are actually watching us like benign hawks.

I stand up. Shake out my limbs. Lean down to drop a casual kiss on Sam's blonde head. And say: 'I promise, Sam. And . . . thank you.'

14

It's happening. It's really happening — exactly the way Cherie had predicted. We are in a tinsel-coated function room with an actual glitterball hanging from the ceiling and the DJ is rocking out the Christmas play-list from hell.

Everyone — including Edie — is dancing in a big circle, kicking their legs and shrieking along to 'I Wish It Could Be Christmas Every Day'.

Everyone apart from me, that is. I am sitting quietly in the corner with a Diet Coke, hoping nobody notices my absence, already feeling a bit overwhelmed by all the 'pampering' we've endured through the day.

I am thoroughly exfoliated, thoroughly buffed, thoroughly moisturised, and thoroughly miserable. There is a room upstairs with my name on it, and I am yearning for my bed.

I glance at my watch and see it is only 10pm. I then glance at the dancing circle, and see that they are showing no signs of tiring. Cherie, Laura, Willow, Ivy and Sophie, and some ladies I don't even know but look like they went to the same School of Rock Chic that Cherie attended — all long hair and reckless abandon and bare feet.

We're at a place called Wildbriar Manor, and it's literally in the middle of nowhere. The grounds are perfectly coiffed and look like they've been pampered themselves, and a light dusting of snow has coated everything I can see through the floor-to-ceiling windows outside. The building is old — the kind of old that comes with mellow stone and thatched outbuildings — and has probably seen a thing or two in its time.

Probably, though, not Edie May — a ninety-year-old dancing queen wearing black leggings, a stick on pink bunny tail and bouncing rabbit ears. Or Cherie and her posse. Or the men, who I know are still outside, drinking in a heated marquee after a day of being macho. It's a strange segregation, and I have a feeling that before the night is out, at least some of the hens and the stags will manage to be somehow reunited.

I am half hoping that they all come back in before the end of the disco, as I would pay good money to see Matt, who can be slightly uptight if Laura's not with him, busting some moves to Slade.

I see Laura herself, flushed with all the dancing — and possibly all the gin and tonics she's been necking — break away from the group and walk towards me. Her hair is flying in wild curls, and her rabbit ears are flapping as she approaches. The pink strand of hair she used to have has now been dyed green, so it will better match the bridesmaid dress she'll be wearing at the wedding in a couple of weeks' time.

She flops down next to me and takes a swig of my Coke without asking. I resist the temptation to stab her in the hand with a fork.

'Uggh,' she says, wrinkling her face up in

disgust. 'It's just Coke! I thought there'd be some Jack Daniels in it. What's up? You don't have to drive anywhere tonight.'

'You never know. I might need to ferry someone to A&E for a hip replacement the way this shindig's shaping up. It's like Glastonbury at a nursing home.'

'Cherie's already been there, done that on the hip replacement, and her new one seems to be bionic . . . I think it'd take more than a bit of bopping to break any of these ladies, don't you? I know this is your idea of hell, but I'm having a ball. Get yourself a proper drink, you'll enjoy it more — or at least hate it less.'

I look at my sister, and try to assess how drunk she is. On a scale of one to ten, I'd say she's only at a six, so I decide — again — to take the plunge. Sam had a point about me not doing everything on my own, and I can only keep my shameful sobriety a secret for so long. Because stupidly, it does feel somehow shameful — not the fact that I'm sober, but the fact that I've never shared any of it with her.

I had my reasons. She was too fragile before, too caught up in her own justifiable grief to be lumbered with anything else. But now? Now she is laughing and smiling again. She's growing. She's found her place in life — and, from the dreamy expression that appears on her face whenever she mentions him, Matt is also proving to be more than adequate in the boudoir department.

She'll never forget David, which is as it should be, but she's so much stronger — maybe strong enough now that I can show a bit of weakness.

'That's the thing, sis. I don't do that any more,' I say, hoping she can hear me above the racket.

'Do what? What thing?'

She looks confused, and I don't blame her.

'I don't drink. I don't do drugs. I don't sleep around. I don't do any of it any more.'

She stares at me, frowning as she tries to register what I've said, the look on her face telling me it simply does not compute.

'I don't understand,' she replies. 'You've always done those things. It's part of what makes you . . . you. Don't get me wrong, I'm not saying they were good things — but . . . why? And when?'

'The day David died,' I answer, simply, giving her a few moments for her mind to catch up with the new reality. The new reality where her crazy, rock 'n' roll party-girl sister has turned into the most boring woman on the face of the planet.

To give her her due, she figures it out pretty quickly. She might spend half her life experimenting with icing sugar, but she's not stupid.

'The day David died . . . ' she repeats, whispering the words. For a moment, the room is quiet, as the DJ eases into the next song. It's blissful right up until the moment that 'Do They Know It's Christmas Time' starts up, and everyone begins to sing along with it. Ah, how I love the festive season.

'You did it for me,' she says, eventually. 'For us. You cleaned up your act because I needed you . . . '

She lays a warm hand over mine, lacing her fingers into my fingers, and I see tears suddenly swimming in the green of her eyes. Irritatingly, the same seems to start happening to me, in some kind of freaky sympathy response, and I blink away the moisture. I. Will. Not. Cry.

'Not just for you,' I say, shaking my head. 'That might have been the initial reason, but now I know it was the best thing for me as well. It probably saved my life, if I'm honest — you know how I was.'

'I do know how you were,' she replies, smiling sadly. 'And I never quite figured it out. It all got so much worse after that Christmas you split up with Shaun. You partied before then, but after that, it all just got so much more . . . self-destructive. And I never knew why. I still don't. What happened to you, Becca?'

'That's a story for another day. Can't do too much sharing in one go, Laura, I've got a rep to protect.'

She smiles and nods, and squeezes my hand.

'All right. I'll hold you to that. I'm still struggling to get my head around this one . . . *nothing?* Really? You don't do any of it any more?'

'Nope. I am Clean-Living Cathy.'

'Is that why you've not . . . you know, Sam? I thought you two were perfect for each other. I sent you all those pictures of him and everything . . . '

'I know you did, and believe me, they were very much appreciated. Just because I'm not in the market to buy doesn't mean I can't

140

window-shop. And Sam is — well, Sam is lovely. A different time, a different place, who knows?'

I find myself gazing out of the windows again as I say this. I know he is out there somewhere. And I know I shouldn't be thinking about him, but I can't really help it. He's somehow crawled under my skin without any effort at all.

'Well, thank you. For doing that. For helping us all when we needed you . . . but . . . '

'But what?' I say, bringing my eyes back to my sister.

'But . . . you can't live like this forever, can you? And I understand what you're saying. And I know that in your mind, you'll have given up everything or nothing. You'll have gone to extremes even in this. You won't have cut down on the drinking, or reduced your romantic liaisons. You'll have cut them all out, at once. That's good — it really is — but have you ever thought about what else you're cutting out?'

'No, but I have a feeling you're about to tell me . . . '

She laughs, and I laugh with her. Each time I make one of these confessions, I feel slightly lighter — less constricted, less trapped by my own demons. Less alone.

'You're cutting out the potential for something good to happen. It's like deciding you're going on a low-carb diet and missing out on all the good stuff in brown rice . . . or something a bit more sexy than that! You know what I mean. I've seen the way you and Sam look at each other. It's hot. It's like, you know in horror films where someone has to kill a zombie or a vampire? And they spray some kind of aerosol in front of them and set it on fire with a lighter? It's like that. Like there's a fire between you. I'm not sure if ignoring that is necessarily the right thing to do, that's all . . . '

I have to grin at her little speech, I really do. She's somehow managed to compare Sam to brown rice and describe my love life as something from a horror movie, and still made sense.

'You may be right, sis. But I'm just getting through life the best I can. I'm trying not to screw up, and that doesn't come naturally to me. And anyway . . . looks like those ladies are calling your name . . . '

She follows my finger as I point to the dance floor, and sees that they have formed a small circle, with someone performing in the centre of it like a comedy version of *Saturday Night Fever*. While we've been chatting, Edie has waltzed with an imaginary partner — probably not for the first time — and Willow has done a spot-on robot.

Now they are waving Laura over, and it's clearly her turn in the spotlight.

She looks back at me, a half-smile on her face, bunny ears sparkling as the disco lights sweep over us. I know part of her wants to just sit here with me and talk this out, but the other part — the part that's made up of gin and tonic — wants to get her party on.

'Go,' I say, gesturing at the laughing women and the sparkling glitterball and the DJ who is creased up laughing as he watches. 'I'm fine. Do that thing Dad used to do where he pretended he was a cowboy throwing a lassoo . . . '

'Or that other one, where he pretended he was bouncing a ball? Or driving a big rig and pulling the hooter?'

'Any of Dad's classic moves will get you a standing ovation. Now shake your tail feather, girlfriend — I have a serious date with another one of these delicious Diet Cokes . . . '

She bounces to her feet and scoots over, just as the DJ starts playing 'Mary's Boy Child'. Cherie clasps her into one of her mammoth Big Mama hugs, and everybody cheers as Laura starts to do her thing.

I see her moonwalk badly around the group, and then segue into a Running Man that bears absolutely no relevance to the music being played, and moves to a completely different beat than the song.

Ah yes. It's definitely beginning to feel a lot like Christmas.

15

I am dreaming of a giant pink bunny rabbit with a machete when I get woken up. All things considered, it's probably a good thing — that bunny did not look fluffy, or friendly. It looked like it wanted to chop me up into little pieces and eat me with a nice Chianti.

I'm happy I've slept at all — perhaps a revelation a day keeps the insomnia at bay, who knows? I'll have to start making things up soon, just so I can get a bit of kip.

I'm not sure what has woken me up initially, and just lie there, still, slightly flustered as the image of the demonic rabbit slowly clears from my mind.

I look around, and see nothing but my hotel room, in shadow apart from the bathroom light, which I've left on with the door pulled to. I've learned that the countryside dark is a lot more serious than city dark, and now tend to leave at least some night-time illumination to stop me from repeatedly stubbing my toes if I wake up.

I let my slightly erratic breathing calm down, and listen. Within seconds, I hear it — tapping on the window of my balcony door. For one second, my heart whoops up and down in fear, somehow convinced that the rabbit is not only real, it's managed to find me . . .

But then I hear my name, whispered, quietly but desperately. Whispered with an Irish accent.

'Becca!' it hisses. 'Are you awake? I'm bloody freezing out here . . . and possibly about to die . . . '

I jump out of bed and do a quick clothing check before I go any further. Yes, I am wearing clothing. Even if it's just a Sons of Anarchy T-shirt that ends above my knees. That'll do, pig.

I walk over to the door and open it. Outside, I see Sam — squeezed onto the two-foot-wide ledge of the Juliet balcony, a look of grim determination on his face. It's the kind of balcony that's made for looking out from or, at the most, sticking a few potted plants on. Not, for sure, the kind that easily holds up six-foot plus of shivering manhood.

His knuckles are white, grasping the rail, and his face is a comical mixture of primal fear and an attempt to look cool. I find his bravado endearing, and stand back as I say: 'You better come in, Sam. But maybe you could have used the other door?'

He clambers over the railing, and lands in a tangled heap of long legs and twisted arms, making an undignified 'oof' noise as he rolls over the carpet.

I close the balcony door again — because it really is freezing out there — and by the time I turn around, he's stretched out full length on the floor, laughing. He's wearing black jeans and a snug white T-shirt that's riding up over his flat stomach, and I avert my eyes.

'Nice nightdress,' he says, looking up at me. 'I didn't realise you were a secret biker chick.'

I realise that he is probably getting an eyeful

from that position, and walk over to the well-used tea-and-coffee-making-facilities to put the kettle on.

'Yep. I ride with the Didsbury Dirty Dogs.'

'Is that a thing?'

'Probably not. Coffee?'

He sits up, and leans against the edge of the bed, nodding. His blond hair is slightly shaggy from being stuck outside in the cold wind and his tanned flesh is goose-bumped. Mine is feeling a bit goose-bumpy as well — for completely different reasons.

I notice that my hands are shaking slightly as I tear the tops of Nescafé sachets and bite down on my lip to try and bring myself back to reality. It's one thing saying no to Sam in the middle of the day — entirely another when he turns up looking long and lithe and luscious in my hotel room in the wee small hours.

'I thought,' he says, grinning at me and running a hand though his hair so it's left in furrows, 'that it would be romantic, you know? I even had a rose in my teeth, but I dropped it once I realised how bloody small that balcony was . . . '

'How did you even get up here?' I ask, sitting on the bed, and throwing the edge of the duvet over my thighs.

'Drainpipe to the first floor, then fire escape to the second. I know, I know . . . not my brightest ever move. In fact utterly ridiculous. But what can I say? You've got me all twisted up in knots. And it was like a scene from a Roman orgy in that ballroom by the time I left . . . Frank and

146

Cherie were slow-dancing to Frank Sinatra, Matt and Laura were snogging under a table, even Frank's grandson Luke was flirting with one of the waitresses . . . and all I could think about was you.'

'I'm sure you could have found yourself some action if you'd tried hard enough, Sam. I mean, you're not exactly ugly . . . '

He laughs, and leans his head against the side of my calf.

'Thanks. The DJ did have a twinkle in his eye, but he's not my type . . . my only type at the moment is you. I keep telling myself to back off. To leave it. After everything you've told me . . . I know I should. But as soon as I've finished telling myself that, I'm outside, figuring out ways to make some big romantic gesture climbing up to your room . . . '

'You're lucky you got the right one. Edie's next door. You'd have given her the fright of her life.'

'She'd probably have decked me with her walking stick. But . . . anyway. I'm sorry.'

'Sorry?' I ask, feeling confused. And feeling, if I'm honest with myself, a little swept away with the sincerity of his words. 'What for?'

'For hassling you. At the very least, for waking you up . . . '

He stands to his feet, and stretches his arms over his head. I notice the edges of the dragon tattoo that I know lurks beneath his T-shirt, along with a purple swirl of bruising.

'What happened?' I say, pointing to the exposed flesh.

He looks down, following my eyes to see what I'm seeing.

'Oh . . . paint-balling. Luke is like, Olympic-level good at it. And Frank might be eighty, but he slaughtered me and Matt. I was on a team with Scrumpy Joe, who'd brought cider with him, predictably enough. He just hid under some camo-netting and got hammered while me and Matt were destroyed. Bloody painful. Feels like I've been driven over by a tractor. I'm probably completely covered in bruises.'

He sits down on the bed next to me, and without being asked to do so, my fingers reach out and stroke the bruised skin. My touch is gentle, but he jerks in response, and one look at his face tells me he's not hurting — he's confused.

'Let me see,' I say quietly, not at all sure where this is going, but apparently convinced it needs to go somewhere. He raises one eyebrow at me and I nod.

He does that cross-armed thing that guys do, pulling his T-shirt over his head and flinging it to the floor.

He's left bare-chested and pretty damn magnificent in front of me. His shoulders are broad and muscled, his body as ripped as I'd seen it on photos over the summer. Photos are one thing, though. The reality is something entirely different.

Bruises are scattered over his torso and sides, mixing in with the ink of the tattoos to create an almost psychedelic tableau of smooth, sun-kissed-skin. He leans back, and his abs ripple, and he smiles — a smile that tells me he knows he looks good, that he's confident without being arrogant, that he will feel every bit as good as he looks.

It's a smile that both reassures me and challenges me. I know I could break this off now, and he'd be fine with it — disappointed, but still Sam. Or . . . I could do what I really want to do. Close the gap between us, touch as well as look. Let him take me away from my own mind. Lose myself in this moment.

He isn't pushing. He's keeping his distance, as though he understands the war that is being waged in my battered brain. He's letting me take control for now, even though I can see — due to having a working set of eyes — that he's as aroused as I am.

I feel something break inside me. My mind flitters back to my conversation with Laura earlier. About how I couldn't go on living like this. About how nobody can survive that level of self-control. About all the extremely valuable nutrients you find in brown rice.

I look at Sam, at the strands of golden hair curling on his bare shoulders. At the uneven breathing shuddering through his body. At the way he is maintaining a gap that I know his every instinct is screaming to close.

I reach out. I run my fingers down his chest, following the ridges of muscle to the waistband of his jeans. I hear him suck in air, and feel his response beneath my hands. And I realise that she was right — and that for me, the moment for change is right here, right now.

'Kiss me,' I say simply, smiling to let him know I mean it. 'I think you've earned it.'

His fingers immediately twine into my hair, and he pulls me into his arms. His lips land on mine, gentle at first. It's as though a fire is lit inside me, inside both of us, and within seconds I am lying beneath him. His knee is between my legs and I am moving against it shamelessly. His hand strokes its way under my top, edging higher and higher until he captures a nipple between his fingers and makes me moan.

He pulls the T-shirt off me, and replaces his fingers with his mouth, sucking and biting at my breast until I am on the verge of some kind of implosion.

I tug at his jeans, desperate now, needing him naked, needing to feel his skin against mine. Needing to feel alive.

He looks at me, pupils dilated, breath ragged, yet still just about in control enough to pause.

'Are you sure?' he asks, quietly.

'Stop talking, Sam,' I reply.

He doesn't need telling twice.

16

When I wake up, I am wrapped in Sam's arms, our legs tangled in the rumpled sheets. Both naked. I take a moment to glory in that, before my brain starts functioning and things get complicated. My brain is a nightmare. I so wish it came with an off switch.

I peek up at him, and realise that he is already awake. He grins at me, so lazily, so utterly charmingly, that I can't help but grin back.

'Morning, princess,' he says, nuzzling into my hair. 'Don't worry, I kept you safe from the killer bunny rabbit . . .'

'What?' I say, momentarily confused.

'The killer bunny rabbit. You were trying to karate chop it in your sleep, telling it to get away or you'd start singing 'Good King Wenceslas' at it . . .'

'Well. That would be enough to scare anything off. I have the kind of voice they include in the highlight reels of the X Factor. You know, those ones where you find yourself wondering if these people have no friends to stop them making tits of themselves?'

'That's okay,' he replies, his hand dusting lightly over my tummy and making me wriggle. 'You have other skills. How . . . how are you feeling?'

Right now, I'm feeling horny again — but I know that's not what he means. We were up for a lot of the night, and there wasn't much talking going on. I had one condom in my bag — which had been there for well over two years, but we were in no mood to question sell-by dates — and for the rest of the time . . . well, we got creative. It's interesting how much sex you can have without actually having sex. I might write a book about it, or at least start a blog.

All things considered, it had been . . . amazing. Like I'd had years' worth of sexual energy ready to unleash. I don't think the poor bloke knew what had hit him. And now, here we are — snuggled up in bed in a strange hotel room, wondering what happens next.

'I'm . . . okay,' I reply, frowning as I try and figure it out. How do I feel? I've been avoiding exactly this kind of situation for so long, and now it feels . . . all right. Better than all right. It feels bloody good, in fact.

'You sure?' he asks, flipping one leg over my hip and tugging me even closer. 'I know you wanted that last night, and I definitely did. But I don't want to be responsible for . . . I don't know, knocking you off track?'

'Don't worry,' I say, letting my fingers drift over the delicious curve of his backside. 'I've not woken up with the urge to do tequila slammers for breakfast, or snort cocaine off your arse. Lovely as it is.'

I give the arse in question a little slap, and he rolls me over onto my back in retaliation. He has my wrists pinned above my head, and his position leaves me in no doubt at all that he's ready to go again. The man is a machine. Which is one of the things I'm very much starting to like about him.

'You know when you climbed that balcony, with a rose in your mouth?' I ask, between taking nibbles of his neck.

'Mmmm?' he replies, not really paying attention any more.

'You really should have brought more condoms.'

'I know,' he says, collapsing down on top of me and laughing into my chest. 'I'm a useless feckin' eejit!'

He is talking with a thick mock-Irish lilt that makes me smile. I stroke his hair, and feel — for just a moment, a rare, rare moment — at peace with the world. I pause, and wallow in it like it's a river made of chocolate.

'So,' he says, clambering off me and lying flat on his back by my side. 'Are you done with me now, Becca?'

'What do you mean?' I ask, fearing he is about to ruin my wallowing.

'I mean, is this it? I know, because you've told me, that you're not a relationship kind of girl. And that's okay — I'd just like to know one way or the other. Because if this was a one-off, I won't carry on hanging round like a lap dog looking for more. I'll just . . . I don't know, join the priesthood or something!'

I elbow him sharply in the ribs, which produces a deeply satisfying 'ugggh' noise. He's ruined my peaceful moment, and he deserved some punishment, but . . . well, it's a fair question. The only problem is I don't really

153

know the answer to it.

'Sam, I've got to be honest here — I don't have a clue. This is uncharted territory for me — actually sleeping with a man I like. Last night was wonderful. And possibly addictive, although that means bugger all with me, I'm the sort of person who gets addicted to jelly babies given enough exposure. I mean . . . I do like you. A lot. You make me laugh. You know a lot about ammonites, which is a particular passion of mine . . . and . . . well. You ain't at all bad in the sack, sir . . . '

'But?' he asks, knowing it's coming.

'But I'm not Laura. I'm not looking to settle. I'm not looking for a life-changing reason to move to Dorset. I'm not looking for the love of my life to whisk me off my feet.'

'What are you looking for, then?'

I throw my hands in the air, and puff out a big, long frustrated breath. Frustration with myself, not anything that he is saying.

'I don't know. Maybe something. Maybe nothing. I'm going home in a few weeks anyway . . . and then this will all feel like a dream sequence in a film.'

'Will you remember me with wavy lines over my face, then?' he asks.

'I will. And wavy lines over all your other parts as well . . . '

I turn to face him, not wanting him to feel bad. Not wanting him to feel like he's woken up with a stranger. Not wanting him to feel like our night together had meant nothing to me — because it had. It had meant so much.

Possibly, if I am entirely honest with myself, too much.

'Sam, I'm a disaster area. You already knew that. It's not like you weren't warned. I'm not the sort of person your mother and sisters would want you to settle down with . . . '

'Jesus, no! And that's probably exactly why I like you so much, Becca. So . . . how about this? We carry on seeing each other while you're here. No pressure. No big conversations. No awkward silences. Just us, enjoying each other, for the time we have left together.'

I consider what he's saying, and examine his face to see if he's sincere.

'Are you offering yourself up to be used, abused and cast aside?' I finally ask, laying a hand on his chest and working my fingers up to his shoulders. Damn, the man is built. It's impossible to think clearly with this much of him, this close.

'Well,' he replies, letting his hands roam in an equally distracting fashion, 'when you put it like that . . . yes. Yes I am.'

He leans forward to kiss me, which is perfect. It stops me thinking, and allows me to simply feel instead.

Things are just starting to heat right up when there is a tentative knock on the door. I ignore it at first, but it comes again — a gentle but insistent tapping.

'Becca? Are you all right, my love?' comes a concerned voice. 'It's half past nine and they stop serving at ten, you know . . . '

It's Edie. I am naked, wrapped in the arms of

my new lover and consumed with carnal thoughts — carnal thoughts that are now being interrupted by a ninety-year-old lady wondering if I'm coming down to breakfast.

I giggle, and Sam's eyes go so wide he looks like a cartoon character.

'Okay, Edie!' I shout, jumping out of bed and away from Sam. 'I'll see you down there!'

I hear her plodding away towards the lift, and stand, hands on hips, looking down at him. Naked. Gorgeous. Spread all over my bed. Mine — for now at least.

'She'll know,' I say, smiling. 'She sees everything.'

'That's true,' he replies, climbing out of bed and rooting around for his clothes. 'But she says nothing. I just hope we weren't too noisy last night . . . '

17

The next week passes in a blur. There are several impromptu shifts at the Comfort Food Cafe, as Laura is in her element with the wedding planning. She's organising the catering, sorting out the band, and co-ordinating the arrivals of several guests.

Among them is Frank's family, his son, daughter-in-law and granddaughter, Erin, who are flying over from Australia for the big event and spending a few days in London first. Also on the list is Brenda, Cherie's older sister, her five children and a scattering of grandchildren, who are all coming down from Scotland on a coach.

One of Laura's big projects over the summer seemed to be specialising in repairing broken families. Cherie and Brenda had fallen out when they were kids, and not spoken for decades before she managed to track her down and arrange for her to come to the café for Frank's eightieth. She also persuaded Peter, his son, to come from Oz with Luke — and Luke ended up staying, working with Matt and Frank and gaining the veterinary experience he needed for his future career. At the same party, I knew she'd also flown in Sam's sisters.

Somewhere along the way, as she was busy healing everybody else's familial wounds, she also managed to start healing her own — with a little help from Matt, Cherie and the children. As I've said before, Laura was made for happy endings. She got all the sugar and spice, and I got the puppy dog's tails.

I've done all the work I need to do for my own clients, as the unofficial Christmas shut-down has well and truly begun, and I am enjoying working at the café, spending time with Willow and getting to know the other customers.

Katie, the bedraggled single mum, and her devil child, Saul, call in most days. I think it fills in time for them, and Saul is always treated like a minor princeling while his mother relaxes for half an hour with tea and toast. No matter what they order, there is an unspoken rule that she only gets charged for a cuppa. I know from Laura that Cherie was left plenty of money when her hubbie died, which is a good thing — because the Comfort Food Café isn't run like any ordinary business. It's more of a social service than a money-making enterprise.

So, I am kept pleasantly busy during the day. If I'm not working, I'm out and about with Midgebo, Lizzie and Nate, who are starting to get excited about the end of term in a few days' time. Lizzie and Josh still seem to be going strong, and I mortified us both by forcing her to discuss the details of their relationship.

I was told, in no uncertain terms, that it was none of my business, that she wasn't stupid, that she's only fifteen, and that I should get my dirty mind out of the gutter. Which was super-fun. It did at least make me rest a bit easier, and cross that jumbo box of condoms off my list of presents for my much-more-sensible-than-me-at-her-age niece.

By night, I am also kept pleasantly busy. Mostly by having fantastic sex. With a fantastic man. Sometimes he comes over to Cherie's apartment, and we listen to her vinyl and eat ice cream and romp around naked.

Sometimes, I go to his little house in the village, where we watch box sets on Netflix and eat ice cream and romp around naked. And sometimes, we go out to secret, quiet places that only he seems to know about — idyllic coves, deserted beaches, hidden caves — where we drink flasks of hot chocolate and watch the stars and don't romp around naked. Because, you know, dead of winter — severe frostbite risk to places you really don't want frostbitten.

So far, so good. My fears that relenting on one of my 'diets' would suddenly result in me falling off every single wagon don't seem to be materialising. Sam is great — if we go out to the pub, he doesn't drink; the same when we stay in.

This makes me feel a little bit weird to start with — like some kind of circus freak that needs to be handled with kid gloves. But I soon understand — because he explains it to me in words of one syllable — that he doesn't mind. That he wants me to feel relaxed. That it's not a big deal. Plus, as he said, 'I don't need booze at the moment — I'm high on all the shagging we've been doing.'

I realise this doesn't sound very romantic to the outside observer, but for me, it is better than a lorry load of hearts and flowers. It's about respect, and kindness, and good old-fashioned lust — three of my very favourite things.

We've not exactly kept our relationship, if that's what you can call it, a secret — but neither are we snogging in public or talking to our Comfort Food companions about it.

This, of course, is driving Laura absolutely bonkers. She is smug beyond belief that she's been proved right; marginally worried about all those wagons I mentioned I was on, and mainly — disgustingly — totally nosy about what Sam is like in bed.

Seriously, she's like a curious schoolgirl about it — being with Matt has definitely opened up a whole new side to her; an earthy side that I've never really noticed before. I'm sure it was there — her and David always seemed to be at it — but perhaps I deliberately distanced myself from it. After all, she was in her perfect marriage, and I was busy working my way through every loser in the North West of England. Not pretty, I know, but true.

I steadfastly refuse to tell her anything at all, which leads to some interesting one-sided conversations where she speculates wildly. She even goes so far as to try and goad me into talking by wondering accidentally out loud if perhaps he has a small willy and that's why I don't want to discuss it. Naughty girl.

Wise to her ways, I simply raise an eyebrow and smirk. Partly I am staying quiet because it is annoying her so much — we are sisters after all, and some habits just don't go away because you allegedly grow up. But partly, perhaps, I don't want to jinx it.

The dark side of me — the side that is still

very much there, and waiting for its chance to leap out and take control, like Mr Hyde lurking in the background — doesn't feel entirely safe. I am allowing myself to be . . . happy. This is a new and unusual feeling for me, and it has taken this thing with Sam to make me realise just how unhappy I have been.

For years, it feels like I have been living in the shadows of my own unsettled memories, punishing myself, lingering on the edge of life rather than plunging straight in. Everything I did that seemed to be fun and pleasurable — the men, the drinking, the partying — was actually just contributing to my private misery.

Now, as I am the very definition of a work-in-progress, I am starting to unravel some of that. I've still not told Laura about the baby, and certainly not Sam — but I've been letting myself at least think about it. Even if it makes me cry, makes me weep myself into a big soggy heap, I've been letting myself think about it. About all that happened then and all that's happened since.

I am starting to understand that the tragedy of it all wasn't just the initial mistake, it was the way I've lived my entire life since then.

I don't know if I'll go back to Manchester as a different person. I have no idea where Sam and me are heading. No clue as to what will happen next — but the one thing I do know is that things had to change. Laura was right. I couldn't carry on like that.

So, against all my better judgement, I am going with the flow. Seeing what happens, and trying to relax as the next stage of my life unfolds around me.

This is a scary thing — and I am terrified.

18

'How about you just drop me off in the middle of nowhere with a compass and a whistle?' I say, sulking next to Sam in the front seat of the truck.

'You wouldn't survive five minutes, city slicker,' he replies, navigating the winding and frost-coated country roads. 'I'd have to come and rescue you before you died of exposure.'

'I don't care,' I answer, genuinely meaning it. 'I really don't want to go to Christmas Blunderland.'

'It's Wonderland. And we're going because Cherie asked us to. Those giant inflatable snowmen won't deliver themselves, you know. What is it with you and Christmas anyway? I've never met such a grinch.'

'I just . . . hate it. I hate the songs and the carols and the fact that Sainsbury's start sending me emails about turkey crowns in November. I hate the Christmas markets in Manchester where everyone is drunk on mulled wine and carrying around wicker reindeers they'll regret buying the next morning. I hate the stupid knitted jumpers and the fake merriment and the way people try and snog you under mistletoe. I hate buying the presents and receiving the presents and wrapping the presents. I hate the forced joviality. I hate the . . . disappointment of it all.'

He snorts with laughter, and I fight the urge to

punch him in the kidneys. That wouldn't be good while he's driving — I'll save it for later.

'Wow,' he says, once he's stopped guffawing, 'that was a pretty comprehensive catalogue of hate, there. But you still haven't explained why.'

I glance at his profile, staying quiet for a second, and wondering if this is one of those moments. You know, those moments where you have a choice. A chance to open up and be honest.

I shake my head, and decide that it isn't. Not just yet.

'Christmas 1991,' I say, simply. 'Some knob of a kid at school told me Santa didn't exist, and I got a Girl's World under the tree, which proved him right.'

'A Girl's World?' he says, frowning, obviously trying to place the name. 'Right! Those fake heads with all the hair and makeup? My sisters had one of those. It had been passed down the lot of them, and by the time it got to Siobahn, it looked like a zombie. Scary as hell. So, what was wrong with that, then? I assume yours was new.'

'It was. But it's not what I'd asked for. I'd asked for Mutant Ninja Turtle toys instead. It was a grave disappointment, and scarred me for life.'

He's laughing again, and I feel a small tug of amusement forming on my own lips in response. Because, you know, when I put it like that it does seem pretty silly.

'And from that one disappointment, you decided to hate everything about Christmas for the rest of your life?'

'Well . . . not just that. But that was the start. It was all downhill from there. I just don't see the point.'

His eyes widen, and I see that, yet again, he is trying hard not to collapse in hysterics. I'm glad I'm of some use. Perhaps I could start a whole new career as a stand-up comedian.

'You don't see the point? Even if you're not religious and don't believe in celebrating the birth of the baby Jesus and all that, the point is . . . well, the point is joy. Happiness. Family. Goodwill to all men.'

'Hmmm . . . I'm not really a goodwill-to-all-men kind of girl, Sam. And anyway, that's another thing I hate — that people start pretending to be all nice with each other, and going to church and doing good deeds, but only for a few days. Then once it's all over, they go back to being bastards.'

I'm warming to my subject, and feeling quite passionate about it by this stage.

'Okay,' says Sam, lifting one hand from the steering wheel and waving it in submission. 'Well, I can see I'm not going to convince you otherwise, so I give up — no need to get your knickers in a twist.'

'I'm not wearing any knickers,' I say, deliberately. This is, in fact a lie. It's way too cold to go commando, but he doesn't know that — and it serves him right for laughing at me so much.

He gulps, audibly, and I see his knuckles whiten as he grips the wheel a bit too tightly. He takes a quick glance over at me, and his blue eyes are sparkling.

'Oh. I see. Well, do you want to pull over and discuss your underwear situation in a bit more depth? There's a little place I know just off the side of the road near here . . . '

Crikey. His brain clearly contains a roadmap of all the potential nookie spots in the whole of the West Country.

'No,' I say firmly, shaking my head. 'I'm far too prim and proper for that. Anyway, I can't wait to get to Christmas Blunderland, I really can't. So hurry up.'

I pat him on the thigh, and look straight ahead, trying not to laugh myself now. He's looking quite uncomfortable, and is obviously thinking naughty thoughts.

'And you'd better stop imagining my underwear situation,' I add, pointing at his lap. 'You'll get arrested if you walk into Christmas Blunderland with that going on. Nobody should find inflatable snowmen that exciting.'

He growls at me and stays quiet for a few minutes. Perhaps he is picturing totally unsexy things like Les Battersby or dentists' waiting rooms to help his self control.

Eventually, we both start laughing, and the rest of the journey passes quickly and pleasantly — until, of course, we arrive at our horror show of a destination.

Christmas Blunderland is exactly how you would imagine it to be, but worse. Everything is covered in glitter and fake holly and plastic icicles that light up, and as you walk through the entrance there's a machine that showers you with pretend snow that is actually tiny bubbles of white foam. I swipe it from my hair in disgust, and mutter a few very un-festive words.

The music is sickly sweet and loud, only rivalled by the excited screams of kids, and the repeated noises made by all the toys that they are playing with — Santas that yell 'Ho Ho Ho', penguins that do 'Jingle Bell Rock'; even a camel that belts out 'Silent Night' in a rich baritone. Someone must have designed that thing, and spent valuable time imagining what kind of singing voice a camel would have. It's a weird world we live in.

The place is packed, mainly with families browsing the decorations and light-up reindeers and giant signs that say 'Santa, Please Stop Here' on them. It smells of a strange combination of real pine trees and all kinds of fake effects, mixed with the aromas of cinnamon, ginger and chocolate wafting through from the café area.

I feel my nose twitch and burst into a rapid-fire sneezing fit. Looks like I might actually be allergic to Christmas after all.

I head to the toilets while Sam sorts out our collection — two ten-foot-tall inflatable snow-men that Cherie wants setting up in the garden of the café, and some kind of special order that comes in about five enormous cardboard boxes.

I stand around looking pretty (or not) while Sam hefts it all into the back of the truck with a member of staff — an eighteen-year-old kid dressed as an elf, complete with pointy green shoes. He has clearly lost all self-respect, as he doesn't even seem embarrassed by this.

By the time we are packed up and ready to go, I feel like I have been trapped in this hell-scape for way too long.

Once we're back on the coastal road and heading towards Budbury again, Sam asks: 'So, how was that for you? Fun times?'

'Not fun times, no. We were stuck there for, like, about three hours.'

'No we weren't, Little Miss Grinch — we were there for twenty-five minutes. I even resisted the urge to browse that magical Christmas toadstool display for you, that's how much I care.'

'Ha! Well, it seemed like longer . . . it all made my skin itch. I could really do with a drink right now.'

There is a marked silence after that, and I realise what I've said. Of course, I know that I don't mean it — that it's just an expression. A way of reflecting my distressed state. A bit like when you say 'I could kill for a mocha right now' in the morning, but you don't actually mean that you'd machete someone down and steal their posh coffee. It is merely a turn of phrase.

But I can tell by the quiet that Sam doesn't understand that, which I get. After I've told him about my demon-battling, what else could I expect? It's annoying, but fair.

'In case your powers of telepathy aren't working at the moment, Sam, I'd just like to stress that I didn't mean that literally, okay?'

He chews his lip, concentrating hard on the road ahead of him, then nods.

'All right. Fair enough. I just . . . well, I know you were worried. Worried that if you started something with me, it would end up with you starting other things as well.'

'I know I said that, but honestly, no. I'm fine. It's fine. Everything is fine. I'm not about to ask you to drop me at the nearest pub and go on a binge. Plus even if I was, that would be my problem to deal with, not yours. And, if we did go to a pub, feel free to have a pint, for God's sake!'

I don't know why I say that. It's petty and mean, especially when I am actually grateful for his temporary abstinence.

'I didn't say you were going to go on a binge, I said I knew you were worried!' he replies, sounding a bit exasperated with me. 'And do you have to be so bloody defensive? What's with all this I-am-an-island crap? Am I not allowed to care about you? Is that it?'

This has gone very bad very quickly, and I feel tears of both anger and frustration welling up as I stare determinedly out of the window at the passing traffic. I am trying not to let any of those annoying tears spill out, but if they do, I don't want him to see.

'Are you crying?' he says, more gently.

'No!' I reply, hoping I don't snuffle. God, what is wrong with me? Dorset has reduced me to a blubbering wreck. I'll be like Laura, crying at John Lewis ads before long.

'I think you are. I have a lot of sisters. When they throw their hair over their face and look to the side like that, it's because they're trying to hide it. I'm sorry, okay? I don't know where that came from . . . I don't want to upset you. I just

169

over-reacted, that's all.'

I shimmy my hair a bit more, because, of course, he is entirely correct. I am now crying, and him apologising and sounding all gentle and concerned isn't helping matters at all.

'Look, it's . . . *fine*. Like I have said, repeatedly. I didn't mean that I wanted a drink. At least I didn't then . . . but I did mean it when I said it was my problem to deal with. Me freaking out about me is one thing. You freaking out about me is another — I am not your responsibility, Sam.'

'What are you, then? My friend with benefits? Or is 'friend' even a bit too much?'

He sounds sad, and that makes me feel sad too. I've hurt him, I can tell. Even if he's not hiding his face with his hair, he's upset. And I don't know how to make it right, and be honest at the same time. In the end I give up.

'Yes, you're my friend. And yes I'm enjoying the benefits. But my problems are my own, and I don't want you worrying about me. I don't like anybody worrying about me. It's too . . . '

'Intimate?'

'Maybe. Maybe I'm the world's biggest commitment-phobe. Maybe I have intimacy issues coming out the wazoo. Maybe I'm an absolute arsehole, But Sam . . . I never pretended to be anything else, did I?'

He puffs out a long, jagged breath, and I can almost feel him controlling what comes out of his mouth next. A skill I've never mastered.

'No, Becca,' he says quietly. 'You never did.'

170

19

When we arrive back at the café, after an uncomfortable silence that neither of us seems able to quite breach, the place is a hive of activity.

Cherie is there, wrapped up in one of those vintage Afghan coats that comes all the way down to the ankles of her moon boots, sitting at a table with Willow and her mum.

Willow's mum, Lynnie, is encased in a padded puffer jacket and is busily arranging what seems to be a vast array of craft activities. She has Alzheimer's and I can't even imagine what that is like for Willow. I know her life is a complex tapestry of carers and work and staying at home with her mother, who sometimes doesn't even recognise her.

Today she seems lucid, and is clearly excited to be there. She used to be the kind of woman who made a living from being arty and spiritual: yoga classes, holistic therapies before they were fashionable, creative workshops for kids, that kind of thing. All of which probably explains why Willow, despite her restricted lifestyle, somehow still manages to come across as a free spirit.

I see that they all have giant mugs of hot chocolate, which Laura is ferrying out from the kitchens on a tray. Katie is there with Saul, and the two of them are helping Lynnie and Willow decorate pine cones. Well, 'help' might be too strong a word, as Saul is mainly using a glue stick to attach glitter to his own chubby cheeks. He is shiny and cute and laughs each time Katie tries to clean him up with a baby wipe. She looks relaxed and happy too, which makes a complete set — just my ugly mug spoiling the festive fun, then.

I walk over to a nearby table, and within seconds my sister has joined me, Midgebo hot on her tail. He's a big, overgrown lummox of a thing now — with the size of an adult dog, but the mentality of a puppy still. I notice that even he hasn't escaped the Christmas craft onslaught, and his shiny black coat is glittering green and red. I smile as he snuffles my hands, licking and nipping as he does a thorough check to make sure I don't have any food hidden about my person. Disappointed, he collapses at my feet with a big doggy sigh, and immediately goes to sleep.

Bella Swan, Willow's Border Terrier, is snoozing with eyes half open at Lynnie's side, wearing a tartan coat and a superior expression. She is one inscrutable dog.

Laura passes me a hot chocolate, the mug brimming over with cream and marshmallows, and I hold it between my hands to warm them up. It's one of those gorgeous, fresh days you sometimes get in December — frosty and cold and clear, bright sunlight streaming down to collide with the sea, the only sounds those of seagulls and us.

Sam is wheeling the boxes up from the carpark on a trolley and unloading them. I look away from him. I'm not really in the mood for admiring his masculine hefting powers at the moment.

'You all right?' Laura asks, straight away.

'I'm fine,' I reply, for what feels like the millionth time that day.

'Really?' she says, concern tinging her voice.

'Definitely,' I answer. 'Maybe.'

She raises an eyebrow at me and I have to laugh.

'Yeah,' I say. 'That's my new thing. I answer all questions with the names of Oasis albums.'

'That's okay. As long as you don't look back in anger . . . '

I pull a face, knowing this could go on all day, and trying very hard to think of a pun that involves champagne supernovas. I come up short, and just shrug. I could say something about cigarettes and alcohol, but that would be a bit too close to the bone right now.

I notice Sam opening the huge boxes with a Stanley knife, and Matt emerges from the café, wearing his Hunky Outdoorsman outfit of khakis and fleece. He's carrying an air pump and a mallet, and looking quite macho. I don't even have to look at Laura to know she's grinning.

'Stop drooling,' I say, 'it's messing up your hot chocolate.'

'I can't help it,' she admits with a giggle. 'There's just something about men with tools, don't you think?'

'I think most men *are* tools,' I reply, sticking my tongue out at Sam in a way that can really only be described as childish.

'Oh dear — trouble in paradise?' she asks, sipping her chocolate and looking at me in a manner that makes me feel like I've just arrived in Guantanamo Bay. She's going to waterboard me with cocoa.

'Nothing to worry about. It's just me and my Christmas allergy. You know how I get. What's in those boxes anyway?'

'I don't know . . . ' she replies, narrowing her eyes at me to say she knows I'm changing the subject, and will not be distracted. Except, of course, she is. We both look on as Sam manages to open the box and holds up . . . well, a pair of shiny white wellington boots.

Each and every box seems to be full of them, in all kinds of sizes. Cherie looks on and claps her hands in glee, way more excited than I've ever seen anyone get about winter footwear.

'Oh!' says Laura, in a lightbulb-going-off tone of voice. 'I think I know what it is . . . Frank says there'll be snow for the wedding. And none of us argue with Frank when it comes to the weather; he's like the unofficial Met Office around here. So, knowing Cherie, she's bought everyone boots to wear . . . '

I shake my head at the sheer insanity of this place. Seriously, stuff happens here that would just never happen anywhere else — and everyone just acts as though it's totally normal. I don't think I'll ever get used to it.

Cherie holds a pair of the boots aloft, shaking them against the sunlight, and sings, loudly and badly: 'It's a nice day for a . . . '

'White wellie!' shout Willow and Sam and,

uncharacteristically, Katie as well. Lord help me. We've moved on from Oasis to Billy Idol. Is nothing sacred?

Cherie laughs her deep, rumbling laugh, the one that seems to make her whole body shake and her grey-streaked plait ripple down her back, and starts to tear them out of their plastic packaging, passing each one to the arts-and-crafts table. Willow and Lynnie promptly get busy with glue guns and glitter and spray-on snow, starting to decorate each of the boots. There are a lot of boots and I suspect they'll be at it for days. Again, I shake my head — I have no words left.

Normally, I'd perhaps find all this eccentricity endearing. But I'm not in the best of moods, and am half wishing I was back in Manchester, watching people puke up kebabs and getting yelled at by lads in souped-up Ford Fiestas who run red lights and listening to the gentle urban lullaby of car horns and sirens and a dozen different languages being gabbled at the same time. Right now, that would make a lot more sense to me.

Even when you're surrounded by people in the city, you can still feel alone there — which I think is kind of what I need right now.

Matt and Sam are busy unfurling the snowmen, and Cherie is telling them where she wants them. I hope they're going to be well weighted down, the wind gets vicious up here when it sweeps up from the bay. I'm also glad that the windows in Cherie's apartment face out to the sea, rather than the garden — I can only imagine the nightmares I'd have if I went to sleep with giant grinning snowman faces looking in on me. The perverts.

'Are you sure you're all right?' asks Laura again, reaching out to pat my hand.

'Yeah. Honest. I'm just . . . really tired, you know? It's making me a bit irritable. Well, even more irritable. Nothing to worry about.'

Even as I say it, I stifle a yawn. It's true — I am tired. Exhausted in fact. Which is really odd, as I've been sleeping better than I have for years. Between the fresh air and the heart-to-hearts and the sex, I've been drifting off easily, and sleeping for whole nights at a time. I should be feeling pumped up and full of energy, and instead I feel like a big lump of play dough, with no shape of my own.

Laura nods and I smile to reassure her. I decide that I will take myself off to bed as soon as I've finished my hot chocolate, and leave this lot to their Christmas-themed madness. Lizzie and Nate will be here from school soon, and I have no doubt that they'll happily spend a few hours spraying boots and helping out. Nobody needs me around, with my negative vibes and low-level misery. They might catch it. It'll be like the Ebola virus of moods.

Partly it's the depressingly unsatisfying conversation I had with Sam, and the way we have left it unresolved. Partly it's just me . . . me being tired. Me being grumpy. Me feeling crowded. Me being me, basically.

We look on as Saul toddles over to Matt, holding out one glitter-glued hand to the half-blown-up snowman. He's wide-eyed and unbelieving as he watches it get bigger and bigger before his eyes.

Matt gestures him closer, and lets him have a go on the air pump. Of course, Matt is doing all the work, but he lets Saul put his tiny foot on the pedal thing with him, pretending that he's doing it instead. With each whoosh of air rushing into the snowman's body, Saul gets more and more excited, squealing and laughing and clapping his hands together. Matt ruffles his tufty blonde hair and I hear Laura sighing next to me.

'He's so good with kids . . . ' she says, leaning her face into her cupped hands, looking completely blissed out. I bite back a retort and just nod. Because while I'm just being me, she's just being her — and that's the way her mind works. She's all about the love and the family and the happiness.

Sam is using the mallet to nail down the long ropes that further attach the snowmen to the ground, and once Saul gets tired of pumping, he goes over to him. Predictably enough, Sam — being the all-round decent guy he is — squats down with the kid, and lets him hold onto the mallet with him. Together, they start banging the pegs in, with everyone cheering them on as they do it.

It is, of course, adorable. And it twists something up inside me so hard I feel like my guts are being tied into knots. If I'd had my baby, he wouldn't be toddling around looking cute any more, obviously. He — or she — would have been practically grown-up by now. Who knows what would have happened? What they might have been like? I'll never know, and suddenly I need to be alone even more than I did before.

'Oh, look,' says Laura, oblivious to my mental state. 'Isn't that sweet? Don't you think Sam will make a lovely dad, too?'

It is exactly the wrong to say to me right now, and she unwittingly pushes me over a ledge I didn't even realise I'd been teetering on. I feel suffocated, stifled, overwhelmed by all the imperfectly perfect people around me, by their happiness and their togetherness and their sugary-sweet niceness.

'You know, Laura,' I say, feeling my own face twist into something angry and unfair, 'I don't have kids. I'll probably never have kids. And I am getting sick of people behaving as though the only way a woman can be judged is by what comes out of her vagina. I'm off to bed.'

I stomp away, not even looking back to see how she reacts. I don't want to know how she reacts. I don't want to see Sam looking gorgeous and fatherly. I don't want to see Katie looking proud. I don't want to see Willow laughing with her mum, or Cherie stalking around the garden like a happy hippie.

I don't want to see any of it. I know I've been a bitch. And I know I'll regret it. But God, I need some space.

20

I wake up with what feels horribly like a hangover — but isn't a hangover — and with what feels horribly like a dog licking my face. Which actually is a dog licking my face.

I screw up my eyes, and sit up. Midgebo takes this as an invitation, and jumps up onto the bed with me. He starts to burrow his way under the duvet, where he takes a very strange amount of interest in my toes. Hey, could be worse.

I let out the world's longest yawn, and open one eye at a time. I'm extremely ashamed of my behaviour yesterday — at least I presume it was yesterday — and am not looking forward to facing the music. I have bridges to build, and apologies to make.

I also, it seems, have coffee to drink.

Sam is sitting on the edge of the bed, holding forth a big, steaming mug of what smells like the good stuff Laura brews up downstairs. I take it from him, and take a small sip before even daring to speak.

'I'm sorry,' I say straight after. 'I acted like a complete cow yesterday. I was really tired and a bit messed up and I took it out on everyone else. I am officially a pain in the bum, I know.'

I am trying to look serious while I say this — because I do one hundred per cent mean it — but Midgebo is tickling my toes so much that I can't help wriggling and grinning at the same time. Sam calls him, and his big, black head pops out from beneath the covers, a confused look on his doggy face. He jumps down off the bed, and goes off to have a good sniff around the room instead.

'It's okay,' says Sam, reaching out to tuck a strand of hair behind my ear. 'I already knew you were a pain in the bum. And I didn't help matters, either. It was just our first row, that's all. It happens to everyone. In fact it's a magical moment, like the first time you fart in bed together, or unexpectedly belch in someone's face just as you're about to kiss them. All part of life's rich tapestry.'

I smile, and wipe the sleep from my eyes. I glance at my watch and see it's after 10am. I have slept solidly for almost twenty hours, and I still feel exhausted. Insomniac, I'm exhausted. Heavy sleeper, I'm exhausted. I just can't win.

'Thank you,' I say simply. 'That's very kind of you. As is the coffee. Is Laura downstairs?'

'She is,' he replies, standing up and whistling to Midgebo, who has found something interesting to chew under one of the chairs. I grimace when I realise it's one of my trainers. Sam follows my gaze, and tells Midge to 'drop'. He does it immediately — some of Matt's training is paying off — and looks up at me guiltily. Damn right he should be guilty. I love my Skechers.

'I'm going down and taking this fella for a walk. I'll give you five minutes to be out of bed and ready to stretch your legs, misery guts.'

'Okay,' I agree, gulping more coffee and shooing him away. If I get out of bed while he's still here, I'll be naked. And if I'm naked, things will start that will definitely take more than five minutes to finish.

Once he's gone, I quickly pull on some jeans and a baggy woolly sweater, my trainers — one of them slightly soggy — and grab my scarf, hat and gloves. These dog walks on the beach are lovely, but bloody cold.

I make my way down the stairs, still slurping the coffee as I go, and emerge into the cafe. Laura is busy creating something that seems to involve 28 metric tonnes of demerara sugar, frowning as she goes. It's her 'mad genius' face, and I know there'll be something delicious waiting when I get back.

I walk up behind her, peer annoyingly over her shoulder, and take a big sniff.

'What is it?' I ask, 'and can I stick my finger in that bowl?'

'It's going to be the sauce for my toffee pudding, and if you stick your finger anywhere near that bowl, I'll chop it off and throw it in the stew.'

I back off quickly. You just never know with Laura when she's in a kitchen state of mind.

She wipes her hands down on her apron, and turns to face me. One strand of curly green hair has escaped its bobble, and lies at the side of her warm face like an alien tendril. She raises her eyebrows, and waits for me to speak. It's not like we haven't done this before — we've done it many times. I mess up, she tolerates it, I apologise. It's one of our favourite sister-act routines. I'm getting tired of it myself though, and resolve to at least try and stop doing things I need to apologise for.

'I know,' I say, holding my hands up. 'I was a prime bee-atch. I didn't mean it, and I'm really sorry. I genuinely was very tired, I'd had a minor disagreement with the surfer dude, and I'd had to go through the doors of Christmas Blunderland to buy giant snowmen. It was . . . Things That Annoy Becca Overload. I shouldn't have taken it out on you, and I really am sorry.'

She is quiet for a moment, biting her lip as she thinks about what I've said.

'That's all right,' she eventually replies. 'You know I forgive you. But are you okay? Really? I mean . . . do I need to be worried about you?'

'Of course,' I answer, grinning. 'What else would you be? I live to keep you on your toes. But no — I'm perfectly fine. And I have a hot date with a black Labrador. Save me some of that sticky-toffee pudding.'

She nods, still not looking completely convinced, but goes back to her baking as I head out to the garden to catch up with Sam and the dog. The dog is busily peeing on one of the snowmen. Luckily Sam isn't.

We make our way down to the beach, and Sam lets Midgebo off the lead. We walk in a straight line along the edge of the water, and Midge runs around in giant squiggles, attacking sticks, pouncing on seaweed, and on one occasion having a romantic interlude with a toy poodle that struts past looking fancy.

Sam and I are quiet-ish, mainly laughing at the dog's antics, occasionally throwing his ball for him, and dodging especially fast-moving waves that sizzle up the sand with surprising speed. It's another freezing-but-glorious day, and quite a few people are down at the beach, with dogs and kids and kites.

It is peaceful and beautiful and perfect, and I make a very unlike-me decision to simply enjoy it all. After about half an hour, we take a break, sitting on a big boulder by the cliff edges and breaking out the coffee flask that Sam, ever prepared, has brought with him.

'Gorgeous, isn't it?' he says, nodding out to sea.

'It is. I can see why you love it here.'

'Can't imagine being anywhere else now. But . . . it won't be quite the same when you've gone.'

'No,' I reply, 'it'll be even better. You'll definitely get a lot more sleep.'

'True. And I won't have to watch any more episodes of *The Walking Dead*.'

'What?' I squeal, laying a hand on my heart as though I'm offended. 'I thought you were loving it?'

'No. I'm secretly terrified every time I have to go and use the loo. And the other day, I saw this guy shuffling around on the beach when I was mending some fences on the coastal path, and I was convinced for a moment he was a zombie.'

'Was he?'

'No. He was just drunk and trying to walk it off before he went home, but I was *this* close to smashing his brains out with a hammer . . . '

He makes a not-very-far-apart shape with his

fingers, and I have to laugh. I'd kind of already known he was scared — he spent most of every episode with his face behind a cushion or making tea — but didn't want to challenge his sense of macho by mocking him for it.

'Well,' I say, slipping my arm around his waist and snuggling up to him. 'You'll get used to it when I'm gone. I suggest you go round to Edie's — she has every series of *Strictly Come Dancing* ready to go, you know . . .'

'Yikes. I think that might be even worse. So, when exactly are you going back, anyway? I'm getting the last flight out to Dublin after the wedding on Christmas Eve.'

'I think . . . some time in the week between Christmas Day and New Year. My mum and dad are coming down for the wedding, which will be an utter delight, so I'll probably stay on a few days after that. But cheer up — I might come back at Easter. I'll bring you an egg and everything.'

'Just Cadburys, please,' he replies, his arm gripping my shoulders. 'I have very common tastes. None of that posh chocolate for me. And I hope you do come back. It'll be something to look forward to.'

'You mean on those long, lonely nights — the ones where you're not down the pub with Matt, or out with Scrumpy Joe, or doing your night-time nature walks, or watching Anton du Beke with Edie?'

'Yeah. On the nights I'm not doing those things. On those nights, I'll be looking forward to seeing you and eating my Maltesers Easter egg. Or Caramel. I don't mind either.'

'That's good to know,' I say, standing up and starting to walk again. We've kept it just light enough for me to start to relax around him again, and that's exactly the level I want to keep it at.

'And in the meantime,' I add, looking at him over my shoulder, 'we have some time left. So let's make the most of it. Last one to that rock over there has to do a striptease to the soundtrack of 'It's Getting Hot In Here' . . . '

21

The big day has finally arrived, and I am feeling suitably nervous. Part of that is because my mum and dad are here, so I feel the need to be on my best behaviour. It wouldn't do to give one of them a heart attack in the middle of the service.

They're staying in their new-but-pre-loved motorhome, which Cherie has let them park up at the Rockery. My parents are interesting people. Interesting in that they appear to be completely boring, but aren't.

My dad, Ken, is a retired engineer, and my mum, Val, stayed at home with us until we were teenagers, when she started working part time in the food hall at the local Marks and Sparks. This resulted in some excellent ready meals for weekend dinners, and as many packets of Percy Pigs as we could eat. Laura once stuffed her face with so many we thought she'd turn pink and start oinking.

On the surface, they're quiet and respectable, neat and tidy, and like nothing more out of control than a game of bingo. They have a big selection of board games, and drive Lizzie and Nate nuts by banning their electronic devices and dragging them around bird sanctuaries and wildlife reserves to see badgers and stuff like that. Every modern teenagers' dream.

But give them a few drinks and they are

completely different people. Christmases, especially, had a tendency to go a bit *Phoenix Nights* on us, especially after Dad bought the karaoke machine. They both like to dance, and would inevitably end up doing some disgustingly smoochy numbers that made me feel a bit sick in my mouth. I mean, no child wants to imagine their parents as sexually active human beings, do they? Even if all the evidence — such as your own existence — suggests otherwise.

They arrived yesterday, and I stayed at Hyacinth with Laura and the kids for the night. Cherie had always warned me she would want to reclaim her little slice of attic heaven for the one night before her wedding, and I suspect she spent it smoking, drinking and listening to music, all on her lonesome. Possibly while wearing a mudpack on her face.

It's a big deal, agreeing to share your life with someone after years of being alone. Her apartment is as close to ideal as I've ever seen for a single woman, and I admire her bravery in giving it all up. In taking that gamble, marrying Frank, moving to his farmhouse — though I wouldn't be surprised if she manages to wangle the odd night back at the café anyway. Some habits are hard to break completely.

There's no doubt they are right for each other. They're one of those couples who are heart-breakingly sweet even when they're just sitting together reading the paper and drinking coffee. And, despite their age, this feels exciting — like a wonderful new beginning for both of them, a second chance after losing their partners.

The atmosphere here is buzzing, and I'm just as infected with it as everybody else — despite it being Christmas Eve, traditionally one of my least-favourite days of the year. There's a background noise of choral Christmas songs, but I'm refusing to let that drag me down. It even sounds quite . . . nice, which is a testament to how good the wedding vibe is.

Frank was right about the weather — of course — and the snow has finally come down properly. It's not dig-your-way-out-of-the-door snowy, but there are several inches layed down on the cliffs and the beach, making them look like they're wrapped up in a big, fluffy white duvet.

The air is clear but chilly, the kind that makes your breath gust out of your mouth when you speak, and the sun is a spectacularly gorgeous shade of yellow, like lemonade pouring from the sky. Matt and Sam and Scrumpy Joe were here early, setting up the chairs, which are arranged in long rows that twist and turn around the various wooden picnic tables.

Some people are sitting next to each other in lines on chairs, like at a normal wedding; others are on the picnic benches, and some are perching on the tables themselves. There are even stools set up around the inflatable snowmen, and someone — I'm guessing one of the Tall Blokes — has been up a stepladder and draped garlands of white and red roses around their fat necks. It's not a conventional set-up, but why would anyone expect that?

I'm trying to hide near the back, because that

is very much my style, and it also means I get a great view of the assembled Budbury masses. I look around and I see that pretty much everyone I've met over the last month is here.

Edie is looking wonderful in one of those old-lady coats with a brooch at the collar and everything she is wearing is pale blue, even her tights. It goes brilliantly with her white wellies.

The wellies are visible on a lot of feet, and have proved to be a very popular addition to the festivities.

Cherie had Lizzie and Nate handing them out at the gate to the garden and I noticed several women shucking off their heels in relief. It's a cafe on a steep hill in the middle of winter — stilettoes just don't cut it. The two of them are pleased as punch to have a job, and they look a bit like ushers at a traditional wedding, but ones that ask your shoe size rather than whether you're with the bride or the groom.

Lizzie looks absolutely stunning in what I can only describe as a little black dress for Gothy teens, a kind of skater fit that she's coupled with thick black tights and Doc Martens. Her hair is long and shiny and straight, flowing golden down her back, and Josh can't stop looking at her. I have to make a conscious effort not to narrow my eyes at him.

She is also taking pictures of everyone as they arrive, and has been buzzing around doing it all day — she's set up an Instagram page for the wedding, and plans to get them all printed out as her gift to Frank and Cherie.

Willow's mum, Lynnie, is sitting with Edie,

looking distracted but not distressed, and the front two rows of the chairs are taken up with the happy couple's family — Frank's impossibly blonde-and-gorgeous tribe from Australia, and Cherie's sister's group. Brenda is smaller than Cherie, but you can see the resemblance. She looks happy to be here, surrounded by her kids and grand-kids, celebrating her sister's marriage. I suppose they have a lot of lost time to make up for.

Ivy and Sophie Wellkettle are here, sitting alongside the Scrumpy Jones family, and perched on the end of their row are Katie and Saul, who is looking super-dapper in a tiny, toddler-sized suit complete with a bow tie that he's already trying to pull off.

Then, of course, there are Budbury's equivalent of male supermodels — or, as they are sometimes known, Matt and Sam. Matt is Frank's best man, and is looking like Han Solo Goes To A Wedding, extremely handsome but slightly uncomfortable in his black suit and tie. Sam is . . . well, Sam is quite a sight to behold.

He's off to one side, manning the sound system, but every now and then his eyes seek me out and he gives me a big, dazzling, dimpled grin. I can see his blue eyes sparkling from here, and he's even had his hair trimmed for the occasion.

He's dressed in the same kind of black suit as Matt, with a smart single-breasted jacket, but he hasn't bothered with a tie. Just a plain white cotton shirt, a few buttons open at the neck. The big advantage of his work wardrobe consisting of cargo pants and fleece jackets is that he looks breathtakingly different now he's all tarted up. Big yums. Even watching him is getting me a bit hot and bothered, and I am having some decidedly wicked thoughts about undoing a few more of those buttons later on. If we can fit it in before he leaves to see his family, that is.

I drag my eyes away from him, and carry on surveying the scene around me.

The gazebo is decorated with endless strands of white and red roses, twined and twisted and draped around the whole structure, so it almost looks as though it's actually part of a beautiful, wild, overgrown garden and not a structure at all.

Cherie has hired loads more patio heaters to dot around, each of them throwing off a warm glow that stops us all from freezing in our seats. Between the flowers and the view down to the bay, it's one of the prettiest settings I've ever seen.

My mum and dad are nearby, Dad wearing the same multipurpose funeral/wedding/Christening suit he's had for at least two decades, and Mum in her very best Per Una ensemble, complete with a lilac felt hat that matches her frock.

Midgebo is with them, being kept still and quiet by Dad's never-ending supply of training treats, which he's sneaking to him every minute or so. If you didn't know, you'd think my dad had some kind of dog hypnosis thing going on — the pup is sitting, tongue hanging out, staring at him with the intense concentration of a sniper setting up his target.

There's a low murmur of chatter against the choral music, lots of laughter, and a sense of real anticipation building as we all keep casting half an eye at the café doors.

Frank, looking dapper in a dark grey three-piece suit, and Matt are under the gazebo, at the table with the registrars. The ladies — Laura, Willow and Cherie herself — are inside somewhere. Cherie has refused to have anybody give her away, stating rather grandly that 'I belong to myself, and I will give myself away.'

I imagine the three of them are in there doing last-minute make-up checks and spritzing each other with perfume, but for all I know, they're downing a bottle of champagne each and telling each other dirty jokes and laughing at keeping us all waiting.

I notice Sam answering his phone and nodding, which tips me off to the fact that we are — perhaps — about to get our first view of the terrible trio.

The doors to the café open, and all heads turn to look. Sam hits a button, and the quiet, dignified, Christmassy stuff ends. It is immediately replaced with new music that starts to pour from the speakers that have been set up on poles around the garden. I definitely wasn't expecting Cherie to go for something like 'Here Comes the Bride', and perhaps had been anticipating some classic rock, a bit of Led Zep maybe. Possibly a bit of Janis Joplin, or Cream.

But, surprising pretty much everyone there, including me, the song now flowing infectiously into our ears is 'Happy' by Pharrell Williams. I hear little Saul screech with delight — I'm guessing he knows this one from the *Despicable Me* movie — and his clapping starts everyone else off as well.

By the time Cherie actually steps out into the garden, pretty much everybody is clapping and singing along, and the mood is awesome. She's not daft, Cherie — she's chosen a song that has put a smile on all our faces. It's impossible to resist.

When she does step out, it's worth the wait. She looks absolutely amazing as she emerges into the garden, Willow and Laura behind her. Her red dress is as beautiful as I remember, and she's wearing some kind of brilliant white faux-fur throw over her shoulders. Her hair is piled up on her head and sprayed with something glittery, and her sparkling white wellies somehow only add to the effect.

Her face breaks out into a huge smile as she sees everyone, and her eyes seek out Frank, who is standing up at the front looking like he just won the lottery. Which he kind of has.

Willow and Laura look almost as good in their green frocks, and Bella Swan trots after them in her green and red coat. All three of the women have gorgeous bouquets: red roses for Willow and Laura, and white for Cherie.

Everyone cheers and roars and stands up as the three of them do a long, circuitous route around the whole garden, so everybody gets a good look at them while Pharrell urges us all to clap along.

Happy, I think, clapping so hard my palms are

starting to sting. It's such a perfect choice — because everyone here looks so very, very happy. Like they've forgotten whatever problems they might have; put aside all their worries for the time being, and are just enjoying themselves, lost in this moment of celebration. Like someone has hit the pause button on real life.

It's really, genuinely lovely, and by the time Cherie joins Frank and the registrar at the table under the flower-strewn gazebo, I realise I have tears streaming down my cheeks.

I swipe them away as quickly as I can, cursing myself for this new-found sentimental streak, and look back up. Sam is watching me from his spot off to the side, and he smiles. I know everyone can see him smile, but I also know that smile was just for me — and it zings all the way across the various heads and hairstyles and hats and hits me smack bang in the heart. Boom.

I smile back, and I'm still crying, and my emotions are all over the place, and I have absolutely no idea what is going on with me.

Maybe it's just because I'm Happy.

22

Everything went off perfectly. Frank recited a poem about second chances and love regained that had us all in tears, and Cherie read out the lyrics to Led Zeppelin's 'Thank You', changing every 'woman' to 'man' as she went. There were jokes about Frank's burnt bacon butties and Cherie's hip replacement, and even the registrars seemed entranced by it all.

Once the ceremony was over and Frank and Cherie were officially declared man and wife, Frank bent his bride over one arm and gave her such a passionate smacker that the whole crowd cheered.

The food was set up inside, and Laura dashes straight from her Matron of Honour duties to start uncovering platters of sandwiches and bowls of salad and huge, warmed cauldrons of soup and stew and chilli, all set up on hot plates.

One whole table was weighed down with nothing but breads, cakes and pastries, and at the centre of it all was the cake — a huge, rectangular affair decorated with a map of Budbury and beyond, with little red icing love hearts at the various places that hold special significance for the couple: the café, Frank's farm, the beach, the pub, and even the hospital where Cherie was taken after her fall.

That last one doesn't sound especially romantic, but it was after her operation that

Cherie went to stay with Frank while she recuperated — and where they both finally realised there was more to their relationship than just being friends.

The menfolk busily clear some of the chairs while everyone else is eating, and the gazebo is transformed from a wedding venue into a stage for the band. Willow has set up a hot chocolate station, complete with giant tubs of tiny marshmallows and a row of squirty cream cans, and Edie and Lynnie have unveiled an entire table full of Christmas arts-and-crafts activities to keep younger guests entertained.

There are quite a few dogs here, not just Bella Swan and Midgebo, and they are either milling around trying to trip people up, or snoozing in the Doggie Play Pen that lives next door to the café — a fenced-in field with sheltered areas, squishy beds and water bowls.

People are milling around between the café and the garden, talking and laughing and eating and drinking, while the band gets set up for Cherie and Frank's first dance and the ensuing party.

I am standing chatting to my mum and dad when Sam walks over to us. I am not a hundred per cent sure how to handle this one — how do I introduce him, after all? I don't have the right words to describe what we have. He's not quite a boyfriend. He's more than a friend. It's . . . complicated. Certainly too complicated to explain to the parentals, so I decide not to even try. I'm pretty sure they'll come to their own conclusions without any help from me, anyway.

We're all holding bowls of food and drinks, and my dad does a weird juggling thing where he manages to shake Sam's hand while also balancing his chilli and pint of Guinness in the other. Crazy skills, forged over years of going to the pub with his mates, I suppose.

Sam is stone-cold sober, as he has to leave before too long to get to the airport, and of course, so am I. Neither of my parents, however, fit into that category, and I see my mother's eyes widen as she looks at him.

To be fair, he is looking pretty handsome. And he does have the accent, which is like a secret weapon where women are concerned. He casually throws one arm around my shoulder as he talks, which intrigues her even further. I can practically see the questions bubbling around in her mind, fizzing about just as much as the glass of Prosecco she's clutching.

After we chat for a few moments — me constantly wondering when Mum is finally going to crack and ask him what his intentions are — Sam says, politely: 'Would it be all right if I borrow Becca for ten minutes? I'm heading back home soon and I just need a quick word with her.'

Of course, they agree, but I can almost feel the pressure of their eyes following us as we walk away. I am smiling, because it is funny — I've never, ever introduced my parents to a man I've been romantically involved with. Sometimes, I barely introduced myself. So now they see me here, with this guy — tall, good-looking, polite, gainfully employed — and must be wondering what the hell is going on. It probably seems like some kind of Christmas miracle.

'Just come down to the carpark with me,' Sam says, grinning at me over his shoulder. He's thrown a big, long woolly scarf around his neck, which looks odd with the suit — like he's dressed as Doctor Who for a convention or something. I guess, from the patchwork colours and uneven knitting, that it was created for him by one of his sisters or nieces.

I follow him down the hill, which has been cleared of snow and gritted, still grateful for the grip on my white wellies, until we reach his van.

His van is a magical wonderland at the best of times — filled with odd bits of rock, sand samples, various tools, bits of netting and plastic sheeting, and random items like binoculars and huge flasks. There's also, I see, as he throws open the doors, a present.

It's chunky and oddly shaped, and wrapped in shiny red paper. He picks it up and hands it to me, smiling shyly. I accept it from him, but then feel instantly guilty not to have anything to give in return. Since things really took off with Sam, I've not been doing a lot of Christmas shopping, which I really should have.

'I'm sorry,' I say, lamely, 'I haven't got you anything.'

I feel really mean now, like an absolute cow, but he just laughs and waves away my apology.

'Don't be daft. I know you don't really do Christmas. It's nothing big anyway. Just send me a picture of your boobs later and we'll call it even.'

Okay, I think, that I can do.

'What is it?' I ask, feeling the edges of the gift — squishy plastic, cardboard, some very weird bumpy shapes. It's quite big, not that heavy and completely impossible to identify.

'It's a watermelon. Look, I'm not going to tell you — that's the whole point of wrapping it up. Just open it tomorrow. I hope you'll like it. Anyway . . . I've got to get off. I've said my goodbyes to that lot up there. I just wanted a moment alone with you.'

He leans forward and kisses me, barely a whisper of his lips on mine. Unhappy with that situation, I grab hold of him and wrap my arms around his shoulders, pulling him in for a more substantial exchange. After a few moments, we both come up for air, and he laughs ruefully.

'I was trying to avoid that,' he says, shaking his head. 'Now I'll have a very uncomfortable drive to the bloody airport, you witch.'

'Serves you right for springing a present on me. And . . . I don't know, happy Christmas?'

It's a pitiful statement, half-heartedly delivered, and doesn't feel right coming from my Christmas-hating mouth. But hey, at least I made the effort.

'Happy Christmas, Becca,' he replies, stroking my cheek in such a tender way that part of me wants to cling onto his ankles and stop him from leaving. 'Thanks for everything, and stay in touch, all right?'

I nod, and realise that I've run out of words now. I'm no longer feeling the Pharrell vibe. I'm feeling sad, and empty, and forlorn as I watch him get in the van, start the engine, and drive away. He toots the horn at me, and I wave, plastering a smile on my face that I just don't feel.

I take a moment, watching him disappear off into the distance, and wonder how I'm going to get through the rest of the party. I've never felt like this saying goodbye to a man before — usually I've felt relieved, to be honest — and I don't particularly like it.

I also don't understand it — Sam has only been in my life for a very short time. How can I already be missing him? Feeling like someone's chopped my arms and legs off and left me stranded and alone? It's completely bonkers, and I am melancholy and confused and aching inside.

I consider walking off down to the bay, trekking along the snow-covered sand until my mind levels itself out, but I hear the sound of extra-loud music wafting down from the café: Cherie and Frank's first dance.

I blow out a big, anguished breath, and make an effort to pull myself together as I trudge up the path, clutching Sam's gift. It's only mid-afternoon, but the sunlight is fading fast, and I see that the endless loops of fairy lights have been switched on, and the whole cafe is starting to look like some kind of fantasy castle perched on top of the cliff.

I reach the gate just as Cherie and Frank take to the 'dance floor' — which is actually just a big, cleared space in the garden. The snow has been shovelled away, and I feel the frosty grass crunch beneath my wellies as I walk.

There has been a lot of speculation as to what their first dance will be performed to. I suspect Scrumpy Joe Jones has even been holding some kind of side-bets on it. Laura's call was 'It's A Wonderful World'. Edie thought it would be 'something lovely by one of those Rat Pack rogues'. Matt suggested they might do the robot to 'I Feel Love' by Donna Summer, which personally I would have paid good money to see. Sam had gone with 'I've Got A Brand New Combine Harvester', which was just plain lazy. I'd been secretly hoping for some Motown magic, or some Marvin Gaye.

It turns out that none of us were right. Of course. If there's one thing I could have predicted, it's that none of us would be able to predict it.

They go for 'My Generation' by The Who, and it is absolutely hilarious.

I suspect this is not quite what Pete Townshend was aiming for, but the song is perfect — and as far as I can see, as I watch Frank windmilling and Cherie shaking her significantly sized, red-satin-enclosed tail feather, Their Generation puts mine to shame.

Everyone jumps in after a minute or so, and within seconds the garden is a heaving mass of drunk people in white wellies, doing scissor kicks and twirls and pogo-ing around. Katie is bouncing Saul on her hip, Willow is head-banging, disappearing beneath of swirl of pink hair, and Lizzie and Nate are off in one corner with the rest of the teenagers busting some deeply uncool moves that they probably intend to be ironic.

I spot Laura and Matt bopping around, looking stupidly happy, and my mum and dad, predictably enough, are in on that action immediately, Dad strutting around like he's Mick Jagger with his chest barrelled out. The effect is spoiled a bit by the beer belly spilling over his suit trousers, but what the heck?

Edie and Lynnie are still making angel-shaped tree decorations with some of the younger children, but I see Edie's wellies tapping away in time beneath the table. Even the registrars are boogying, as this was their last 'gig' of the day.

Everyone looks daft and none of them care. Just the way it should be at a wedding. I get brief flashes of Frank and Cherie at the centre of it, her red dress glinting and her hair now loose and wild. Frank's bunch from Australia are dancing together, and quite a few of Cherie's relatives are cutting loose as well.

They are completely surrounded by love: sisters, children, grandkids, nieces, nephews and, just as importantly, their friends.

I am smiling at what I can see, but a tiny bit of me is dying inside. I walk towards the cafe, where I can pretend to be eating, but where, in reality, I know I can be alone.

I have that feeling again.

The one I used to be so used to. The one I had that first night I celebrated with these people — the one where I am on the outside looking in. I realise that I've been getting used to being free of it; that for some time now, I've actually been part of this world, not just an observer. I've been living life right alongside them, and now, suddenly, it's all drained out of me. As if by evil magic.

The only difference I can identify in my circumstances is that Sam is gone, but I refuse to accept that I am quite that pathetic. That the only thing connecting me to Cherie and Frank and Edie and Budbury and my own bloody sister, for goodness' sake, is a man I've known for less than a month.

It's got to be more than that, but I can't quite grasp what. I am tired, as usual, and I am overly-emotional. Tears never seem to be far from the surface at the moment, and I am going to miss Sam — all of them — so much when I go home, no matter how much I try to deny it to myself.

Maybe this is my way of coping. Maybe my usually twisted-up little defence mechanisms are kicking in, and my head's decided I need to disengage with Dorset before I do myself some real damage. That sounds mental, even to me — which means it could well be right.

For everyone out there, in the fairy-lit garden with the flowers and the snow and the music and the inflatable snowmen, the party has just begun.

For me, it feels like it's over.

23

I am woken up the next morning by my niece very deliberately bouncing up and down on the bottom of my bed. Or, to be more precise, her bed — she bunked in with Nate for the night to make room for me.

The motion of the mattress wobbling around is making me feel decidedly queasy, and I clutch my stomach, head still hiding beneath the duvet. I only fell asleep what felt like minutes ago, and am not ready to face the world just yet.

Lizzie, of course, has other ideas. I peek out from the covers and see that she is wearing a pair of Kylo Ren pyjamas. Cool.

'Come on! Come on! Come on! It's CHRIIIIIIIIISTMAS!' she yells, like a deranged teenaged Noddy Holder. 'We've been waiting for you to get up for ages — you need to come and see if Santa's been or not!'

'Lizzie,' I mutter, using scissoring motions to try and kick her off the end of the bed, but only succeeding in looking like my legs are being jolted by a taser, 'you are fifteen. I know you don't believe in Santa any more.'

'I know, I know . . . but I'm trying to preserve my sense of child-like wonder. You guys are always telling me not to be in such a rush to grow up!'

She is, of course, evil. Because, yes, we do say things like that.

'I've changed my mind,' I grumble, trying to roll myself back up in a ball. 'I want you to grow up immediately. Go out and join the army or get married or whatever . . . just leave me alone . . . I need to get some *sleep* . . . '

'Well, tough,' Lizzie replies, snatching the covers off me and throwing the duvet to the floor. I am left there exposed and suddenly cold, wearing saggy old PJs that are nowhere near as cool as hers.

'You've got to come down. We've opened our big presents and now we need to do yours. Plus I need to use you as a diversion — Gran and Granddad are here, and they keep talking about going for a 'constitutional'. I think that means they want us to go outside, and that's not on my list of things to do today. I want to stay in, eat myself stupid and play with my toys.'

'Toys? Do you still get toys?' I ask, reluctantly admitting defeat and staggering around the room looking for my dressing gown. 'What, like, Ker Plunk or something?'

'No, don't be daft,' she says, handing me exactly the thing I was looking for — who knew I'd actually been organised enough to hang it on the back of the door? — 'I mean technology, obviously. A new laptop. Which of course I desperately needed for *school* . . . '

The tone of her voice indicates that, in fact, she will be using the laptop purely for watching videos of kittens, stalking Josh and messing around on photo-sharing sites.

'What about Nate?' I ask, glancing in the mirror and immediately regretting it. I look

205

awful. My hair is stuck flat to my head on one side and sticking up in tufts on the other. My skin is pale and blotchy, and I have dark circles like bruises beneath both eyes. It looks like I've been punching myself in the face while I slept.

I decide it doesn't matter — I am among friends — and follow a skittering Lizzie down the stairs, as she chatters away telling me Nate got a new guitar and some X Box games, and I focus mainly on not tripping down the steps. It wouldn't be the first time I've fallen flat on my face on Christmas Day, but I'm hoping that's all behind me. I'm still feeling queasy from Lizzie jumping up and down on the bed, though, and it's not being helped by the smell of cooking wafting up from below.

I'd half expected the Comfort Food Café to actually open on Christmas Day, and for Laura and Cherie to throw open their doors to all the waifs and strays of Budbury. But Frank and Cherie have so many family members down for the wedding, they decided to just book the same hotel they had their stag-and-hen night in so everyone could have their own space, and they'll all be eating their Christmas lunch there together.

Tomorrow, the two of them are going off for a few nights alone in Cornwall, before flying back to Australia with Frank's family. Maybe Cherie will end up opening a Perth branch of the Comfort Food Cafe and never come back. Who knows?

Our Christmas gathering will consist of me, Laura and the kids, Matt and Midgebo, Mum and Dad, and Edie May. Laura invited Katie and Saul, but apparently Katie was happy with a 'quiet one' this year.

As I walk through into the lounge, I am relieved she said no — Hyacinth really isn't that big, and it's going to be a tight squeeze as it is. I'm already feeling crowded and Matt and Edie haven't even arrived.

Mum and Dad are sitting next to each other on the sofa and Dad is trying to play some kind of FIFA X Box game with Nate, who is sitting cross-legged on the carpet. Dad is frowning very heavily, and waving the controller around while he frantically presses random buttons. My nephew, by contrast, is sitting very calmly, and using his superior thirteen-year-old video gaming skills to make his Messi run all the way to goal.

The fake crowd goes wild, but Dad makes a harrumphing sound and drops the controls onto the sofa cushion. He's not happy. I can predict almost to the syllable what he will say next.

I see Laura in the kitchen, already getting me a mug of coffee, and our eyes meet across a crowded cottage. She raises her eyebrows at me, smiling, and we both mouth the words: 'When I was a lad . . . '

'Bloody stupid game, if you ask me,' Dad says, crossing his arms over his chest. He's wearing his Nice Christmas Shirt today, which will have been purchased new for him by my mum. 'When I was a lad, we used to be outside playing the real thing, not sat in twiddling our thumbs . . . '

I bite back the laughter, and instead go and give them both a kiss on the cheek. I ruffle

Nate's hair, and perch on the arm of the couch.

'Don't worry, Granddad,' says Nate, ever the diplomat of the family, 'we'll go out and have a proper game later. Matt'll come with us, and Aunt Becca will join in, won't you?'

'Course,' I say, gratefully accepting the coffee Laura hands to me. 'Just be prepared to lose.'

I can actually think of pretty much nothing worse than running around at the moment, except perhaps eating a huge turkey dinner while wearing a paper hat from a cracker. Sadly, both seem to be on the horizon, so I need to suck it up.

Laura plonks herself down on the armchair, and wipes her curly hair away from her face. She looks a little flustered and a bit red-cheeked, which tells me she's probably been happily tinkering away in the kitchen for hours already. I have a sudden and uncharacteristic surge of guilt at being such an anti-Christmas auntie, when everyone else seems to be up for it.

My sister catered a wedding yesterday — and now she's cooking Christmas dinner. I know she loves it, but still . . .

'Is there anything I can do?' I ask, the steam from the coffee billowing in front of my face as I speak. 'Peel carrots? Chop parsnips? Do whatever it is you do to sprouts?'

'No, don't worry,' says my sister, grinning at me. 'I'd actually like the food to be edible. Why don't you open your presents?'

I nod, and smile, and try to look excited, and she laughs. She knows I hate this, and I know that she knows, and she knows I know she knows . . . and, well, you get the picture. There's a whole lot of knowing going on.

Lizzie and Nate are actually pretty keen on this part, obviously, and start to pass me parcels up from the bottom of the ginormous Christmas tree. It's been shedding so much there is a light scattering of pine needles over all the gifts, and I also see that the lower branches have definitely been nibbled. Probably by a naughty black Lab puppy. They'd only been able to put the presents out yesterday, as Midgebo was staying with Matt — he'd completely torn to shreds the one and only package they put there earlier, obviously sensing that there was a highly delicious and apparently edible (to a Labrador) set of matching coasters in there.

'This is from us,' says Lizzie, as I take one of the presents from her hands. I squeeze it and shake it and blow on it, in a charade of trying to figure out what it is, and eventually just rip off the paper. It doesn't even have the chance to hit the floor before my mum has grabbed the wrapping up, screwed it into a ball, and placed it neatly in the black bin bag she has on her lap. She's a house-keeping Ninja.

Inside the parcel is a T-shirt. I open it up and see the words 'Bah Humbug!' printed with big, black capital letters. It makes me laugh, which delights the kids, and Lizzie immediately makes me pose holding it up for the camera for a photo.

Next, they present me with a giant Walking Dead mug — 'for your morning coffee, Auntie Becca' — and a toiletry set that is apparently designed to help you sleep. It seems my foibles have not gone unnoticed. I make happy noises and take a sniff of the lavender bath oil. This is a mistake, as it is so strong I almost gag.

I manage to hide that by immediately gulping down more coffee, and urging the kids to open their gifts from me.

The next half an hour or so has a certain rhythm to it. We take presents from under the tree, and tear the paper off them. Mum demonstrates a supernatural ability to catch and dispose of said paper, no matter how far out of her reach it seems to be. We all proclaim ourselves delighted with our various items, which is definitely more true in some cases than others.

I, for example, am genuinely pretty taken with the photo frame that Lizzie and Nate have made for me — shop-bought but decorated with shells they've collected from the beach. There is also a small envelope full of printed pictures from throughout my stay, which is very sweet.

I look quickly through them, but am horrified to find that they are making me well up — so I simply pick the first one I see of Nate and Lizzie, and decide that will be the one for the frame. I slip it behind the glass with shaky hands, and hope nobody notices I'm an emotional wreck.

Lizzie and Nate seem pleased with the very carefully chosen presents I give them — they each get a gift-wrapped box inside a gift-wrapped box inside another gift-wrapped box, the smallest one containing £50. Cash: the most personal gift a teen can get. I've also given Lizzie a nice book on photography, which she seems enthralled by, and a chess set made out of Marvel super-heroes to Nate.

Laura gives me a big box of Roses, and I give her a big box of Quality Street. This is an established ritual that we've been following since she had Lizzie, and we decided that our lives were too busy for shopping.

There is, of course, also the Princess Leia slave-girl outfit, but that's not one to open in front of our parents. It would either lead to a shocked silence, or, even worse, my mum saying 'I've got one just like that at home, haven't I Ken? It doesn't half chafe, though . . . '

My mum and dad, as ever, manage to get things that are awful and yet hilariously perfect. Lizzie pretends to be delighted with her new Britney Spears perfume, and Nate can barely keep his face straight when he unwraps a Lego set. Laura gets a *Guide to British Birds* — 'because I know you've been keen on those skylarks in the garden' — says Mum, proudly. I am the lucky recipient of a £30 voucher to get myself Hopi ear candle-d.

By the time we've finished, it's getting towards midday, and Laura has decided everyone needs 'some snacks.'

This, in the Incredible World of Laura, can mean anything from opening a box of mint Matchmakers and passing them round to a full cheeseboard, home-made truffles and 15 different types of stuffed olives.

We usually eat our 'proper' dinner at about 4, which leaves us plenty of time to slump in front of the TV for an hour or so, clutching our stomachs and groaning, until someone — usually Dad — decides that 'a bit of a sing-song' might be called for.

In previous years, I've found a way to leave after dinner — at least until David died, that is. Since then, I've made a point of always sticking around, no matter how hard it's been. I always felt I had to, because Laura and the kids needed me.

This year, I think, listening to her humming Christmas carols to herself in the kitchen, I'm not sure she needs me at all. I glance at Lizzie, and she is busy with her laptop. She's doing intermittent typing, pausing, and smiling, which tells me she's probably messaging Josh. Nate is immersed with his new guitar, strumming away in the window seat, watching out for Matt, his own personal guitar hero.

Mum and Dad are now playing each other on the FIFA game, which is hilarious. Neither of them knows what they're doing, so the footballers are just running backwards and forwards and falling over, kicking chunks of grass instead of the ball.

I decide that I need to go and get dressed — I am the only adult still in nightwear — and to get my phone. I should text Sam, wish him a happy Christmas. Open the present he got me, which is still in my bag.

I'm feeling a little less deflated than I was last night, but still not good. Physically I'm not a hundred per cent, and emotionally I'm on the numb side. It's as though a wall has gone up again, blocking me off from other people, from this blissful unreality of Budbury life. I know it's almost time for me to go home anyway, so I need to stop being a big baby, get through the rest of the day and basically fake it till I make it.

I stand up from my perch on the arm of the sofa, just as Laura walks through with a big wooden platter full of minced pies and a jug of cream. She lays it down on the table, goes back to the kitchen, and brings over some lattice-topped pork pie and a small bowl of chilli chutney. Obviously, if this was my house, it would have been bought from Sainsbury's. Well, even more obviously, if it was my house, none of it would be happening.

But as it's Laura's house, everything is home-made and perfect and looks divine. She's sprinkled sugar on top of the still-warm pies, and the smell is wonderful.

I walk over to the table, ready to grab myself a small plate — by which I mean an enormous plate — full of yummy goodness, when suddenly I don't feel so great. I've been a bit off all morning, and was putting it down to lack of sleep, the excitement of the wedding, or possibly the three bowls of chilli I ate during the course of the wedding.

Whatever it is, it's bad. Wave after wave of nausea hits me, and I run to the downstairs loo, only just managing to make it before I fall to my knees and puke my guts up. I don't even have time to pull my hair back properly, and I can't say that I care.

I'm there for a good few minutes, wretching until there is nothing left in my stomach apart from watery bile. It's utterly disgusting, and even worse, I seem to have done it all with an audience. And I don't just mean the framed photo of Jim Morrison from The Doors that Cherie has on the wall in here.

Laura comes up behind me, kneeling next to me and putting her arm around my shoulders. I try to push her away — I don't want her getting messed up, plus I'm actually a bit embarrassed.

I have no idea why — it's not like these people haven't see me vomiting before. It's not like all of them, apart from the kids obviously, haven't at some point or another looked on as I've collapsed in this exact same position, doing this exact same thing.

They've all held my hair back; they've all dabbed my clammy forehead with a damp cloth; they've all handed me wads of tissue to clean myself up with. My mum, I know, has probably also snuck into my room at night to check up on me, make sure I'm still alive.

Once you've been the daughter who gets brought home drunk by the police on Christmas Day, you've crossed a line that can never be uncrossed.

I look behind me, and see my mum and dad peering at me over Laura's shoulder, Lizzie and Nate hovering somewhere in the background. Through my tear-blurred eyes, I instantly recognise the expression on my parents' faces.

It's the one that I know so well. It's full of pity and love and concern and also exasperation. Disappointment. Resignation. The sure knowledge that no matter how much they hope otherwise, Daughter Number Two will always be the one who screws up.

I use the tissue Laura passes me to wipe my

mouth, and lean back, so I'm sitting on my heels. I feel dizzy and a bit spaced out, and like I might be sick again any second.

Usually, I know the drill. Paracetamol. Diet Coke. Bacon butty. Half a day in bed. But that's the cure for my long-lost hangovers — and unless someone was slipping me secret vodkas in my cranberry last night, this isn't a hangover. This is something entirely different.

The thing is, none of *them* know that, do they? My parents have no idea that I'm Sober Barbie not Party Barbie these days, and Laura's only known for a little while. I can tell from the worried face she's pulling, and the way she's murmuring as she tries to console me, that she is probably assuming that I fell off the wagon last night. That I was so heartbroken at Sam leaving that I looked for relief at the bottom of a glass.

For the time being, it's beyond me to try and convince them otherwise. The weight of their collective anxiety is too much for me. It was bad enough when my behaviour warranted it — now it's even worse.

I use the sink to pull myself up to my feet, and splash my face with cold water. There's not much room in the downstairs loo, and Laura backs out to give me more space.

'You all right?' she asks, quietly, reaching out to smooth down my tufty hair. Mum is chewing her lip, and Lizzie is frowning at me, looking possibly the most worried of the lot of them. Enough, I decide, is enough.

'I'm fine,' I say, as firmly as I can with my insides still feeling like rubber, 'just an upset tummy. I feel much better now. I don't know who cooked that chilli last night, but I may complain about the chef to the local council . . . '

Laura lets out a 'ha!' noise, and Lizzie laughs faintly, and my dad nudges my mum, as if to say 'look, she's all right — she's making a joke!'

The tension falls down several notches after that. A joke is a joke, no matter how crap it might be. Once they all seem relieved that I'm not going to need a lift to A&E to get my stomach pumped or anything, I manage to escape their cloying concern, almost crawling up the stairs to get a shower. Nobody argues, as it is blatantly clear that I do, in fact, desperately need one. My dressing gown probably needs to be incinerated as well.

I bag all my yukky clothes up to get washed, or thrown away, and wait till the temperature is just right. I take my time, sitting down in the bath and letting the water pour over my head for a few blissful minutes. My stomach still feels crampy and even the thought of food is enough to make me gag, but at least I don't have clumps of puke in my hair. Even I have standards.

After I'm as clean as it's possible for a human being to be without isolating themselves in a sterile bubble, I wrap myself up in a towel and sit on the edge of Lizzie's bed. I hear the door open downstairs and the sound of Matt arriving, shouting his greetings. He's accompanied by Midgebo, who, guessing from the cries of the humans, proceeds to dive around the room rummaging in bin bags and trying to eat chocolates and generally causing all kinds of canine chaos.

I can picture it all: Matt and Laura on their best behaviour in front of Mum and Dad, but still catching a quick smooch under the mistletoe hanging from the kitchen ceiling; Nate playing his guitar; Mum and Dad sucking at FIFA; Midgebo peeing on the Christmas tree; Lizzie taking photos of it all. And later, when Matt's been to collect her, Edie May, my all-time hero, nibbling at her Christmas lunch and taking home an extra portion for 'her fiancé'.

I'll miss them all, I think, as I drag myself into clean clothes and stuff the few things I have with me into my backpack. The rest of my stuff and my laptop are still at Cherie's place, so I'll have to stop off there as well.

Still, I can be on the road within an hour or so, I think, glancing at my watch. I peer out of the window, and see that although the surrounding fields are still white with snow, it's stopped falling at least.

I'm planning how best to say goodbye to everyone when there's a small knock at the door. Laura pops half her head around, one eye wide as she sees me dressed and packed up. She walks in, and sits next to me on the bed. She's brought all my Christmas presents up for me, and she lays them down on the pillow.

I am partly expecting a lecture, or at least an attempt to persuade me to stay, but instead, she just takes one of my hands in hers and gives my fingers a squeeze.

'Just to Cherie's, or all the way to Manchester?' she asks, quietly.

'All the way, I think . . . I'm sorry . . .'

'It's okay,' she says, smiling. 'I understand. I'm amazed you've lasted this long!'

'I know, right?' I reply, feeling pathetically grateful for her understanding. 'I did good. Almost a whole month. I just . . . I just need to go home. I need to be on my own for a bit.'

'I get it,' she answers, pulling me in for a proper cuddle. 'There's no need to explain. It's been brilliant having you here, and I know you'll be back.'

She's taking this so calmly, so well. It makes me realise that I was a hundred per cent right earlier — she doesn't need me any more. She'll never forget David, but the days of her living in the land of the nervous breakdown are well and truly gone. She's not even the 'old' Laura — she's a new, improved Laura; stronger than ever.

'I love you so much,' I say, when she finally lets go of me. 'I don't say it often enough.'

'I don't know . . . I think maybe you said it in 2010?'

'Was that during my home-brew phase?'

'I think it was.'

'That explains it, then . . . anyway. I do. Thanks for having me, sis. Thanks for letting me into this lovely world of yours. I'm so happy you came here, and met Matt, and all of the people here. The kids are doing so well, aren't they?'

She nods, beaming with pride. She's right to be proud, I think. Not just of them — but of herself as well.

'Do you want to sneak off?' she asks. 'I'll say you went to the drop-in centre, or got eaten by

Godzilla or something?'

'I think the Godzilla story will go down better . . . but, yeah, if you don't mind. I'll give you all a bell when I get back up North, and Mum and Dad will be home later in the week anyway. Plus, you know, it's not like anybody expects me to be anything other than bonkers, is it?'

I'm getting dressed as we speak and pull on the Bah Humbug! T-shirt with my jeans. It seems super appropriate right now, as I'm about to bunk off Christmas.

'Well, you never let us down on that front, Becca,' says Laura, standing up and wiping a sneaky tear from her eye. 'On any front, actually — don't write yourself off as the crazy one all the time. You've got me through more rough patches than you know. I couldn't have done this — made this move, started this new life — without you. You're my sister, and you're ace, so stop slagging yourself off. I just won't have it.'

'Aye aye captain,' I say, giving her a little salute as I pack my gifts up. 'And make sure you give Edie a big hug for me, will you? Tell her I'll be in touch.'

She nods, and I turn to leave, jogging quietly down the stairs. I pause and look through into the living room for a moment, smiling at what I see. Everyone looks happy. They'll barely even notice I'm gone.

I'm just about to make my dramatic escape when Midgebo gallops through, and sticks his muzzle up my bum. Because dogs are nice like that. Luckily I'm wearing jeans, so it's not quite as invasive as it could be.

219

Matt follows the dog through, and I see that he has fallen foul of the Paper Hat Fairy already. His chestnut brown hair is poking out of the sides of it, and he's looking at me quizzically. If he really was Han Solo, this might be one of those times he says 'I've got a bad feeling about this . . . '

'Shhh!' I say, holding one finger to my mouth. 'I'm running away! Laura knows — she's upstairs. She might need a cuddle. Oh, and if you look in the carrier bag second drawer down, you'll find something special. Call it a Christmas present to both of you . . . '

Matt nods, and gives me a very brief hug. He's not a touchy-feely kind of man with anyone other than my sister, so I appreciate the gesture.

'Okay. Right. Come back soon. I expect you will. Laura didn't even make it past the M5 when she tried to leave . . . '

'Well,' I say, standing on tippy-toes and giving him a quick kiss on the cheek, 'that's because she had you waiting for her back here, isn't it? She's not daft, you know. Look after her for me, won't you?'

'I'll look after all of them, don't worry,' he says, and I believe him.

I close the door quietly behind me, and hope they enjoy the Princess Leia costume.

24

I am sitting at the nearest decent-sized service station, sipping coffee and looking out at an especially un-festive scene. It's surprisingly busy here, maybe with people visiting relatives or possibly running away from relatives.

The pure, dazzling white snow on the fields around Budbury is just a fading memory now — the snow here has been driven over, had oil dripped on it, dogs peeing on it, and hundreds of trudging feet kicking it about. It's a grey and yellow slush, which is just about perfect for my state of mind.

I'd called in at Cherie's and packed up all my stuff, hastily scribbling her a note saying thank you and trying not to cry as I said my farewells to her attic sanctuary. I'd miss all the crazy decorations and the posters and the amazing view down to the bay.

It was quite melancholy, locking the café back up again, dark, completely empty, and still in chaos from the wedding.

There's a Boxing Day clean-up planned, but for the time being, the room still looks sad. The leftover food has been thrown away or taken home by guests, but the place is still strewn with decorations, wilting paper plates, half-full glasses, stray confetti and the coloured stuff from inside party poppers.

Outside, all the electrical gear and the heaters

and the extra chairs have been collected by the hire company, and there are numerous bin bags full of rubbish tied up and placed under tables, the plastic making ruffling noises in the breeze.

The inflatable snowmen are looking a bit worse for wear, sagging in the middle as though they have a tummy bug, and the flower garlands around their necks are hanging off and blowing around. There are several random white wellies scattered around, as though someone threw a load of them in the air and they landed at odd angles in odd places. It's the Party That Time Forgot.

I escaped as quickly and as painlessly as I could, texting Laura to let her know I was on my way back home and would speak to her when I landed. 'All good here', she texted back, 'Mum and Dad drunk and singing 'Footloose'.'

I respond with a smiley face. By which I mean a smiley face emoji, obviously, as my real face, the one on the front of my head, isn't feeling quite so smiley.

I go back to my coffee, and try to dredge up the will to do what I need to do. I am feeling very sick, in all kinds of ways. And I'm not stupid. Well, not entirely stupid. I have, at least, watched lots of TV shows and films with women in them.

And in those films and TV shows, as soon as a woman is sick — especially in the morning — it means they're pregnant. It's one of those signifiers, isn't it? I mean, the woman is never sick because she ate a dodgy kebab, is she? Or drank a whole bottle of Jack Daniels? It always means she's up the duff.

Of course, I could just have a tummy bug, like the inflatable snowmen. That would be a normal thing to happen — and as I am not a woman from a film, that's far more likely. But at the back of my mind are a few doubts, niggling away at me.

Like that first night with Sam, where we used the prehistoric condom from my bag. And the fact that as well as feeling sick, I've been so very, very tired, and extremely emotional. Seriously emotional — like, enough to make Gwyneth Paltrow's Oscar speech look heartless.

It was one of the reasons I needed to get away — to have some time to myself to find out the truth. Laura didn't seem angry with me anyway, but at least I can, at some point, explain to her what was going on, so she knows that I had a good reason to be doing a runner.

I'd called at an open pharmacy on the way here, and am now all set to resort to everyone's modern day GP — Dr Google. I quickly type in the words 'morning sickness', and get about six million hits. I click on the first one that doesn't look as though it's been written by morons, and my mind is immediately put at rest by the first sentence.

Morning sickness usually comes on at about week six of a pregnancy, I read. Which is something of a relief, as that can't be the case with me — I hadn't even met Sam in the flesh six weeks ago. Virile a man as he is, there's no way I could have got preggers by looking at a photo of him.

The second sentence, though, is a bit more slippery. It stresses that every woman is different, and in some cases, it can start as early as a few weeks in. Hmmm. Feeling a bit less relieved now.

I sip some of my coffee, which tastes like I'm drinking lighter fluid, and decide that there's only one way to find out for sure. I'm also dying for a wee, so at least the coffee was good for something.

It's funny, I think, as I grab my backpack and head for the ladies, how Laura and I seem to have significant moments at service stations.

It was here that Laura finally decided not to come home to Manchester, and turned the car right back around, setting off with Nate and Lizzie to start their new life in Budbury. And now I'm heading off to pee on a stick. Must be a family trait; something hereditary like a tendency towards asthma or ginger hair. Service Station Syndrome. I resist the urge to Google it and see if it's real, because I know I'm just stalling.

I make my way through the sparse but miserable-looking crowds, taking in the unhappy faces of the staff and the now quite sorry state of the decorations. Ah, Christmas. It'll all be over soon, and the world will go back to normal. Or not.

Within a few moments, I am sitting uncomfortably in one of the stalls, rooting around in my bag with my thighs crushed up against one of those plastic sanitary bins next to the loo.

I read the instructions, do my business and stare at the framed poster on the back of the toilet door. It's an advert for a product that claims to help with female incontinence, showing a ridiculously happy lady with very white teeth. She seems strangely thrilled to be tinkling in her pants to me.

While I'm waiting, I notice that Sam's present is still sitting in my bag, unopened. What the heck, I think, I might as well go for it — at least if it makes me cry, I'm tucked away in private.

I tear off the shiny red wrapping, and am at first confused by what I see. Because it is an unexpected gift for a fully grown woman in her thirties. It is, in fact, a complete set of Teenage Mutant Ninja Turtle action figures. Just like I'd wanted all those years ago.

It is so sweet. So thoughtful, and funny, and so just like Sam to remember, that I do in fact burst into tears.

Then I look at the pregnancy test, and cry even more. I don't know if I am crying from happiness or sadness or sheer delirium. But I do at least know one thing now.

I am definitely pregnant.

PART 3

Christmas Future?

25

It is New Year's Eve, and I am having a little party all by myself. I've settled back into my flat, which at first felt cold and alien when I arrived home.

To be fair, I was feeling pretty cold and alien myself by that stage, having battled my way along several motorways in foul weather, in a state of emotional and physical disarray.

I'd emerged from the service station toilets into a completely different reality, and it was going to take a bit of getting used to.

Since David's death, I like to think I'd become a lot less selfish, putting Laura's needs before my own, and generally working hard to develop the All Round Good Egg aspect of my personality that had been sadly neglected for many years.

But concentrating on supporting your grieving sister and her children is a whole lot different than the situation I was facing now.

There were so many different scenarios: have the baby and raise it alone. Have the baby and move to Dorset to be with Sam. Have the baby and go and live with my mum and dad. And, of course, the most troublesome option — not have the baby at all. That one floats around in my mind for a little while, and I let it, even though I know that ultimately it will be rejected.

That said, there's no use pretending this is an ideal set-up. This was as far away from a planned pregnancy as it was possible to be, and logically my life as it is now simply won't cope with motherhood.

There are the logistics, like the fact that I'm self-employed, have no financial security, and live in a small one-bedroomed flat in Manchester city centre. That I know bugger-all about babies, and once in fact tried to feed Nate a bag of Chilli Doritos when he was five months old. That I might be doing this alone, and I'll struggle to keep my already tenuous grip on normality.

That I have absolutely no idea if I can do this — if I can be a mother at all. I mean, I even kill houseplants. What chance would a tiny human being have?

I've spent the last week trying to answer at least some of those questions. I am the proud owner of a box of pre-natal vitamins; a multi-pack of ginger tea bags, and a copy of *Parenting for Dummies*, which is a real thing you can buy off Amazon and everything. I have crossed the word 'dummies' off the front in black marker pen and written 'Becca' on it instead. Though I suppose the two words mean exactly the same in this situation.

I've cleaned the flat, stocked up on healthy food and done a preliminary check to see how many plug sockets I'm going to need to buy covers for. You know, in a year and a half or so.

All of this, of course, indicates to me that the option of not having the baby definitely isn't going to fly. I got a taxi to the clinic a few days ago, and when we went over a speed bump, I found myself clutching my stomach protectively.

I know by this stage, even though I haven't told anybody, that I am going to keep it, no matter how much of a dummy I am.

At first, it felt scary. I'd be loading up the dishwasher, and suddenly wonder how I'd do that with a tiny baby attached to my boobs. I had to stop, and sit down with a sketch pad, and work out some basics techniques — baby carrier, bouncy chair, keeping it in some kind of moving box . . . which, once I thought about it, could be described by some people as a 'pram'.

I'd be walking up the stairs to my flat with my shopping bags, and ask myself the same question: how would I do this with a baby, even if I did have a really good moving box to store it in? There's a lift, but it's not always working. I'd need a jet pack, maybe, or the ability to teleport. But how would that affect the baby? Would it be able to reassemble all its various blobby cells back where they needed to be, or would it end up with an ear on its big toe? These were issues never fully explored on *Star Trek*.

So, I've done a lot of thinking. Mainly about strange random crap like that. What I've not done, and what I know I need to do very soon, is start talking to people about it. People who can help, like Laura. And people who need to know — like Sam.

He's texted a few times, and called. I've not responded, apart from one little line saying I was home and safe and thanks for the pressie, because . . . well, because I'm a dick, I suppose. He's done nothing to deserve the silent treatment, and this is a classic case of 'it's not you, it's me'.

I needed this week, alone, to get my head around things. To start feeling physically more robust. To try and come up with some kind of plan for the future.

Planning for the future has never been my strong suit, and I don't seem to be getting any better at it. Apart from deciding I need a jet pack and twelve plug-socket covers, that is.

Also, I think, I wanted this week to just . . . enjoy. Be happy. Make the most of this time where it's only me and the tiny creature that has taken up residence inside me. Before I involve Sam and my family.

I realise that it's not a proper baby yet. It's a tiny blob, like frogspawn or something. But it's mine, and I feel a fierce and protective love for it that I've never experienced before.

That's not quite as straightforward and joyful as it sounds. Because this newfound love, this precious happiness, is tinged with sadness as well. With regret. With grief. With the ever-present 'what ifs' that always swamp me when I cast my mind back to my teenaged years, and the baby I lost. The baby I thought I didn't want.

It would have been awful losing a baby at any stage — but the fact that for all these years, the pain of it has been tainted by my own self-loathing makes it even more bitter. As though — and I know how crazy this sounds — that child knew it wasn't wanted; that it somehow felt my confusion and fear and ambiguity.

It's bonkers, but I can't quite let it go. I have to live with it, and I have to make up for it — and this baby, this new life that Sam and I miraculously and accidentally created, will be the most loved child the world has ever known.

I decided this morning that I will tell Sam tomorrow. I don't know how that phone call is going to go. Something along the lines of: 'Happy New Year! Hey, guess what? You're going to be a daddy!'

It will be a shock, and I'll need to give him time to process the idea. I won't make any demands on him, and I'm determined not to create any drama around it all. And he's Sam — he's lovely. He's solid and caring and funny and wonderful. I am, I know, as much in love with him as it's possible for me to be. If not for the baby, I'd be missing him like crazy, and wondering how insane I am to have left at all.

He might not jump for joy initially, but I trust him enough to know he also won't say or do anything that will leave me lying in a heap of crumpled tissues wishing I'd never told him.

Before then, though, before I change his life forever by telling him, I'm going to have my party. Me and little Binky. This is my pet name for the baby. It may well end up being the real name for the baby as well, who knows?

I sit back, surveying my party supplies and hold my hands over my belly. There's a baby in there. A real-life Binky. I still can't quite believe it, and I still can't quite believe how happy it's made me. I've never yearned for kids. I've never felt maternal. Never pined away for what Laura has.

But now, I think perhaps that somewhere along the line — sometime after my teenaged disaster — I simply squashed down that part of me. Or drank it to within an inch of its life, shut it up so it wouldn't keep nagging at me. Partied it out of existence, telling myself it just didn't exist.

These days, though, a party is a very different thing. These days, a party consists of a small dining table piled high with cranberry juice, sliced strawberries and dipping chocolate, and a big bowl of cocktail sausages. Okay, so I'm not quite Laura on the catering front — but it's the best I could do.

The only problem is, my appetite still isn't back to normal, and I have to sprint for the toilet at the drop of a hat — I may end up simply looking at my party table, or possibly throwing up all over it. It's the thought that counts.

It's about 11pm now, and I am desperately hoping that I will make it through until midnight. I'd like to sit out on my tiny balcony, wrapped up in Sam's khaki fleece which seemed to make it into my suitcase and still smells of him, and watch the fireworks explode all over the city. Just me and Binky, partying on down. We might even invite Jools Holland if we're feeling sociable. Although, I suspect, already stifling yawns, we might also go to bed before the party even starts.

I've just dipped my first strawberry when the buzzer on the intercom goes off. I mentally slap myself round the head for forgetting to turn it off. It's New Year's Eve, and the streets are full of idiots. I'll have random strangers pressing the button and asking if they can use my loo or wait for a taxi or get changed out of their Pikachu outfits if I leave it on.

I'm just about to flick the switch when it buzzes again. Annoyed, and slightly concerned it might actually be someone I know — someone from my past life calling to see if I fancy a pint or ten — I hit answer and snap a quick 'hello'.

'Hey Becca — any chance of letting a passing Irish man in for a cuppa?'

26

I jump back from the intercom panel as though I've just been electrocuted. In fact, it feels like I have.

I'd decided to tell Sam tomorrow. Him turning up my doorstep tonight was not part of the plan, and I don't know quite how to react. Bizarrely, I look in the mirror, which is possibly the girliest thing I've ever done. I even fluff my hair up a bit, and wipe a smudge of chocolate off my cheek. There's nothing much I can do about the outfit though: flannel pyjamas that are probably as old as Edie.

He buzzes again, and I realise that I've not even let him in. I press the enter button, and know I have about two minutes maximum before he's knocking at the front door. I spend most of those two minutes hiding the pre-natal vitamins and the baby book. I want to actually tell him the news, not have him figure it out and feel like I've been trying to hide it from him. Which I have, kind of, but only for a little bit.

I manage a quick spray of perfume just before I open the door to the flat, which for some reason makes me feel much better. I may look like crap. I may feel like crap. But I smell damn fine.

Sam is standing in the doorway, all tall and gorgeous and smiley and twinkly-eyed. His blonde hair is curling over the collar of his jacket, and I just want to eat him. Seriously, just gobble him all up.

Of all the reactions to seeing him again that I'd anticipated, this wasn't it. I expected to be nervous. To be anxious. To maybe even be a little bit resentful.

What I didn't expect was to be absolutely overwhelmed with . . . what? Relief? Lust? Happiness? A combination of all of those? I'm not quite sure, but whatever it is, it feels right. I have no idea why he's here, standing on my doorstep, but I am one hundred per cent sure that I'm glad he is. Huh. Weird. Looks like I actually *was* missing him like crazy; I just hadn't realised it.

'So?' he says, grinning at me. 'Are you going to invite me in?'

'Hang on — are you a vampire?' I reply, dragging him in by the lapels. 'Do you need to be invited in?'

'Um . . . I can be a vampire if you want me to . . . ' he says, laughing as I wrap my arms around him and pull him in tight. He's cold, which is no surprise as he's been outside. Where it is, you know, freezing. I rub my hands up and down his back and kiss his jaw and make cooing noises and generally behave like a lunatic. He seems to enjoy it, and returns the compliment by nuzzling into my hair. God, I'm so pleased to see him. And I'm so glad I sprayed that perfume on.

'Now, not that this isn't lovely and all, but . . . what's going on? You don't call. You don't write. You don't like my pictures on Facebook. I was beginning to think you'd gone right off me,' he says, laughter in his voice.

'No!' I reply, finally letting go and standing back to look at him. He has a backpack with him, and the smart black pea coat he's wearing is new, so I assume it was a Christmas gift. 'I've just been . . . well, busy. Weirdly busy. Busy with stuff I want to tell you about. Anyway . . . why are you here? Aren't you in Ireland?'

'No,' he says, dumping the bag and unbuttoning the coat. It's a very nice coat, but I'm happy to see him taking it off.

'I'm apparently not in Ireland. I got back from Dublin yesterday, and nothing much was going on in Budbury. So I just, you know, decided to pay you a visit . . . I didn't call ahead because to be honest, I thought you might tell me not to come. I didn't hear from you much over Christmas, and Laura said . . . well, she said you'd taken off. I was . . . look, don't go nuts, but I was a bit worried about you, all right?'

I don't blame him for saying that. The last time he implied he might be worried about me, I did kind of go nuts.

'I'm good,' I say, feeling the first hint of nerves creep in now the excitement of seeing him is fading. In fact, the excitement of seeing him has made me feel even more nervous.

Before, I'd somehow convinced myself that I could do all of this without Sam. That I wanted to do it without Sam, even. Now, with him standing in my flat, so tall his head's almost touching the ceiling, looking the way he looks and just being so . . . so *here* . . . I realise that I don't want to do it without him. I don't want to do anything without him.

What if he doesn't feel the same? What if he's just here looking for a quickie, no matter what he says? What if he freaks out and runs off screaming into the night? What if, what if, what if . . .

'Are you okay?' he asks, taking hold of my arms and holding me steady, his blue eyes boring into mine. 'You look like you're going to be sick. Did I do the wrong thing? Do you want me to go?'

I stand tall, and kiss him firmly on the lips, letting him know that I really don't.

'I want you to stay,' I say, but then dash away from him, as quickly as I can. Talk about mixed messages. I shout over my shoulder: 'But you were right about me being sick!'

When I come back out, several minutes and one very thorough tooth-brushing later, he's lounging on the sofa, his long legs stretched out in front of him. He has a plate of cocktail sausages on his lap, and has made himself right at home. I collapse down next to him, suddenly very tired.

'Sexy, huh?' I say, not even daring to look at the sausages.

'Damn right. What's going on? Have you got a tummy bug or something?'

He slips his arm around my shoulder and snuggles me into him, which, considering he thinks I am probably contagious right now, is a very sweet thing to do.

'Um . . . no. I know it doesn't look like it, but

I'm actually feeling great. I have something to tell you, and I don't want you to freak out, and I know it's going to be a shock, and I hope you're not going to be sick yourself when I tell you, and it's a big deal, but — '

'Are you pregnant?' he says simply, putting his plate down on the coffee table and turning round to look at me.

Wow. Talk about stealing somebody's thunder.

'Yes,' I reply, marginally narked that I didn't get to make my big announcement. 'With quintuplets,' I add, out of spite.

He bursts out laughing, and I get the feeling he doesn't believe me about the quintuplets after all.

'So . . . how did you know?' I ask, not at all sure what's going on here. 'And how do you feel about it?'

'You do remember how many big sisters I have, don't you?' he says, stroking my hair and kissing my forehead and generally wrapping me up as tight as he can.

'There was always someone throwing up in my ma's house. And you were . . . I don't know. A bit emotional? And tired. Tired and pissed off, and crying. And now randomly puking. Pregnant woman behaviour, basically. So . . . I suppose we have to talk about this, don't we? I mean, I'm assuming you were going to mention it, at some point?'

'I was. Tomorrow. I was going to call you and tell you tomorrow. I wasn't hiding it, I only found out on Christmas Day myself, and I just needed to . . . sort it out. In my brain. Don't be angry with me.'

'I'm not angry,' he replies, resting his chin on the top of my head. It's weird. I can feel his jaw move through my skull as he talks. I don't mention this, as it is a strange thing to be noticing right now.

'I can understand why you needed a bit of time, and that's fine, don't worry,' he says, slowly. 'And did you come to any conclusions? Did you sort anything out?'

He is keeping his tone very, very neutral and I'm not quite sure what that means. His body language — arms around me, thighs crushed next to mine, full-contact cuddling — says he's happy, but his voice says nothing much either way.

I pull away a little, so I can actually look him in the face and see what he's thinking. Or, I decide, as I take in his perfectly lovely but deliberately bland expression, maybe not. Oh God. Maybe he's not happy after all.

'I did sort a few things out,' I say, quietly, feeling my lower lip tremble like the lower lip of the Biggest Wuss in the World.

'Mainly, I figured out that I want to keep this baby, Sam. There's a lot I need to tell you, about me and why I am like I am, and this isn't the time for it. But . . . I want it. Very much. If you don't, then I understand. Really. I do. There's no pressure, and if you want to leave right now, I won't be upset with you.'

'Really?' he replies, reaching out to stroke my cheek with his thumbs. 'Then why are you crying?'

'I'm not crying!' I insist, even though all the

241

evidence suggests otherwise. 'And, honestly, I know this is big news. I don't want to trap you. You can go back to Budbury and I can do this on my own. I won't ask you for money, or time, or anything at all . . . '

'Ah,' he says, as though he's just figured something out. 'I see what you're doing.'

'What am I doing?' I ask. 'Apart from allegedly crying.'

'You're doing that Becca thing where you're trying to push me away yourself, before I get the chance to do it to you. A kind of pre-emptive rejection, because you're already assuming the worst.'

I want to disagree, and do at least manage to frown. But he has a point. That kind of is what I'm doing.

'I thought you looked a bit . . . neutral. Not happy.'

'I was looking neutral for your benefit, you daft cow,' he says, leaning forward and kissing me. 'I didn't know what you'd decided, and if you weren't keeping the baby, I didn't want to pile on the guilt.'

'So . . . you *do* want this? Or you do if I want it? Or you don't . . . Sam, I'm confused!'

He rubs his hands over his face in frustration, and I feel a wave of sympathy for the man. I mean, I even frustrate myself sometimes. I can only imagine what it's like to be on the outside of my brain looking in.

'Okay,' he says, grabbing both of my hands in his and holding them still on his lap. 'Let me make it simple for you. I — Sam Brennan

— love you, Becca Fletcher. I want this baby, and I want you. I've never wanted anything more in my entire life. Now. Is there a way you can misunderstand that, or is it clear enough?'

It is clear. It couldn't be more clear. And yet there is still something stopping me from quite believing it.

'But it's so complicated,' I say, even annoying myself. The man's just told me he loves me, and wants our baby, and I'm still whining. 'You're in Dorset. I'm here. What will we do?'

'What we'll do is figure it out,' he replies, smiling. 'You'll move to Budbury, or I'll move here, or we'll shack up halfway between both.'

'You can't move here. Where would you go surfing?'

'I don't know — the Manchester Ship Canal? Look, it doesn't matter. That's just the detail. The small stuff. It's nothing that we can't fix. The big stuff? The stuff that matters? That's right here. Just me, you, and this baby.'

He touches my tummy gently, and I place my hand over his. He's right. Of course he's right. Big picture.

'It's called Binky,' I say, grinning at him.

'Of course it is,' he answers. 'Best name ever. Now, would Binky and yourself like to celebrate New Year with me? It's almost time . . . '

I glance at my watch, and see there are only minutes to go until midnight. I stand up, too quickly as it turns out, and have to spend a few moments waiting for my stomach to return to Planet Earth.

'Come on,' I say, leading him towards the

243

balcony. 'We can watch the fireworks out here.'

I grab his fleece from the chair, and wrap myself up in it. He raises his eyebrows at me, and I say: 'I stole it. It smells of you, and I've been wearing it every night. Have you got a problem with that?'

He shakes his head, and holds up his hands in a 'whatever you say' gesture as he follows me out to the balcony. He brings the cranberry juice and a couple of glasses, and settles onto the bench next to me.

It's extremely cold, and our breath billows out of our mouths and clouds onto the dark night air. I can hear the sounds of parties and laughter and car horns and a thousand slightly off-kilter countdowns from the city below us. It's not like Budbury here — everything is lit up, neon silvers and golds, rivers of light flowing along the roads, noise from every possible angle.

Midnight seems to be struck at about five different times, and various versions of 'Auld Lang Syne' start to drift up towards our perch. At least the first bit of it does — nobody ever remembers the words past the first bit, do they?

It's not the Jurassic Coast, for sure, but it is pretty, in its own way.

I turn to Sam, and he passes me a champagne flute full of juice.

'Happy New Year, Becca,' he says, raising the glass in a toast. 'And to Binky as well. I can't wait to meet her.'

'It's a girl, then, is it?'

'Definitely. I can just tell. And I'm good with girls.'

244

That, I have to admit, is true.

'You are,' I reply. 'I can't deny this. And Sam . . .'

'Yes dear?' he asks, pretending to sound like an old married man.

'I love you.'

'I know,' he says, giving me a wink and stealing one of Han Solo's best lines.

'Is it all going to be okay?' I say, feeling a bit spaced out by everything that's happened.

'It's going to be better than okay. It's going to be brilliant. You're just going to have to trust me on that one.'

I smile. I drink some juice. I let one hand rest gently twined in his, the other on Binky. I watch the fireworks.

And I trust him.

We do hope that you have enjoyed reading this large print book.

Did you know that all of our titles are available for purchase?

We publish a wide range of high quality large print books including:
Romances, Mysteries, Classics
General Fiction
Non Fiction and Westerns

Special interest titles available in large print are:
The Little Oxford Dictionary
Music Book
Song Book
Hymn Book
Service Book

Also available from us courtesy of Oxford University Press:
Young Readers' Dictionary
(large print edition)
Young Readers' Thesaurus
(large print edition)

For further information or a free brochure, please contact us at:
Ulverscroft Large Print Books Ltd.,
The Green, Bradgate Road, Anstey,
Leicester, LE7 7FU, England.
Tel: (00 44) 0116 236 4325
Fax: (00 44) 0116 234 0205

SUNSHINE ON A RAINY DAY

Bryony Fraser

It's Zoe and Jack's first wedding anniversary, and they've got an announcement: they're getting divorced! Marriage isn't for everyone — something that Zoe and Jack discovered only *after* they'd walked down the aisle. Bad timing, huh? So now they're stuck together in their once-harmonious marital home, neither of them willing to move out. With Zoe's three sisters always wanting a say, and Jack's best friend trying his hardest to fix things between them, misunderstandings arise. Tempers flare. 'Accidents' happen. But maybe things aren't quite as final as they seem?

RUSHING WATERS

Danielle Steel

As Hurricane Ophelia bears down on New York City, millions are caught up in the horrific flooding it unleashes. Interior designer Ellen Wharton flies in from London, heedless of the hurricane warnings, intent on seeing her mother. British investment banker Charles Williams is travelling on business but is also eager to see his young daughters, who live with his estranged ex-wife. As the hurricane rages, he desperately checks the shelters where thousands have taken refuge to find them. Juliette Dubois, a dedicated ER doctor, fights to save lives when the generators at the hospital fail. The day of chaos takes its toll as New Yorkers struggle to face a natural disaster of epic proportions. But as lives are shattered, heroes are revealed — and then the real challenge begins, when the survivors face their futures . . .